The Scientist

Katrina Calleja

ISBN-10: 1499730357
ISBN-13: 978-1499730357

DEDICATION

To Adrian, for your love.

To my family, for your support.

And to Sam, for your strength, courage and laughter.

CONTENTS

CONTENTS

BIBLIOGRAPHY, RESOURCES
ACKNOWLEDGMENTS

Books

Johnson, Steven Berlin. *The Ghost Map: The Story of London's Most Terrifying Epidemic and How It Changed Science, Cities, and the Modern World.* New York, Riverhead Books, 2006.

Lodish H, Berk A, Zipursky SL, et al. *Molecular Cell Biology.* 4th edition. New York, W.H. Freeman, 2000.

Mukherjee, Siddhartha. *The Emperor of All Maladies: A Biography of Cancer.* New York, Scribner, 2010.

Newitt, Malyn. *A History of Mozambique.* London, Hurst & Company, 1995.

Journals

Edwards, Andrew M. and Massey, Ruth C. *Invasion of Human Cells by a Bacterial Pathogen.* Can. J. Infect. Dis. Med. Microbiol. 2006 Sep-Oct; 17 (5): 297–306. PMCID: PMC2095089.

Froman Seymour, Will Drake W., and Bogen Emil. *Bacteriophage Active against Virulent Mycobacterium tuberculosis—I. Isolation and Activity.* J Assoc Physicians India. 2003 Jun; 51:593-6.

Kropinski Andrew M, PhD. *Phage Therapy – Everything Old is New Again.* Antimicrob Agents Chemother. 2001 March; 45 (3): 649–659. Doi: 10.1128/AAC.45.3.649-659.2001. PMCID: PMC90351.

Mathur MD, Vidhani S, Mehndiratta PL. *Bacteriophage Therapy: an alternative to conventional antibiotics.* J Assoc. Physicians India. 2003 Jun; 51:593-6.

Parracho HM, Burrowes BH, Enright MC, McConville ML, Harper DR. *The role of regulated clinical trials in the development of bacteriophage therapeutics.* J Mol Genet Med. 2012; 6:279-86. Epub 2012 Apr 23.

Símboli N, Takiff H, McNerney R, López B, Martin A, Palomino JC, Barrera L, Ritacco V. *In-house phage amplification assay is a sound alternative for detecting rifampin-resistant Mycobacterium tuberculosis in low-resource settings.* Antimicrob Agents Chemother. 2005 Jan; 49 (1): 425-7.

Sulakvelidze Alexander, Alavidze Zemphira, and Morris J. Glenn, Jr. *Bacteriophage Therapy.* Am J Public Health Nations Health. 1954 October; 44 (10): 1326–1333. PMCID: PMC1620761.

Vogelstein, B., Sur, S. & Prives, C. (2010) p53: *The Most Frequently Altered Gene in Human Cancers.* Nature Education 3 (9): 6.

Historical documents

Hankin M.E. *The bactericidal action of the waters of the Jamuna and Ganga rivers on Cholera microbes.* Ann. Inst. Pasteur 10:511–523 (1896).

General News and Science Websites

http://www.pharmaphorum.com
http://www.ncbi.nlm.nih.gov/nucleotide/35213
http://www.explorecuriocity.org/content.aspx?contentid=2530
http://eliava-institute.org/
http://www.dairyscience.info/index.php
http://www.bio.davidson.edu/people/dawessner/302/302Lab6.html
http://www.cancerquest.org/p53-function.html
http://p53.free.fr/index.html
http://www.mrsaphages.com/
http://www.spvm.qc.ca/en/
http://www.eurosurveillance.org/ViewArticle.aspx?ArticleId=1159
http://www.who.int/topics/tuberculosis/en/

Videos

BBC *Horizon* Documentary Program:

"Defeating Cancer," Series 48, Episode 14; 2011-2012
"The Virus that Cures," Series 34, Episode 3; 1997-1998
"Defeating the Superbugs," Series 49, Episode 6; 2012-2013

A special thanks to SGT. W. Minnear.

CHAPTER ONE

Swallowing back the metallic taste of dried blood, Richard Sinclair clutched at the stabbing cramp in his side as he launched himself through the elevator's open doors.

His clenched and sweaty fist landed hard against the lone white button at the top of the stainless steel panel. And with only his racing heart to fill the void of anxious silence, he waited for the elevator doors to close. But nothing happened. Again and again he pounded on the button, but still the doors would not close.

Narrowing his eyes, he blinked and gave his head a shake. And as his trembling limbs gave out, he staggered back, bracing himself against the elevator's mirrored walls. The button he had been pounding on was not a push button at all, but rather one of the large white buttons from a *Hudson's Bay* coat he had worn as a child.

He froze as a bright red light suddenly flashed from behind the button. Four beams shot through its thread holes, projecting onto his chest like tracer fire. An eerie chill shot from his toe nails to his fingertips, leaving the sensation of curdled blood in its wake. Too terrified to blink, he resisted the involuntary reflex until dryness forced his lids to meet. Swallowing hard, he inched toward the doorway.

Now standing with his feet butted against the raised metal track, his bulging eyes fixed on the institutional clock directly opposite. And though the clock's thin black arm did not move, its ticking echoed menacingly in his ear. The footsteps were getting closer.

1

His gut told him to run, but fear-borne indecision kept him frozen in place.

A cold draft suddenly washed over his sweat soaked brow. He tilted his ear toward the ceiling, toward what sounded like the whistle of wind through leafless trees. Sound's warning preceding sight's confirmation, he heeded the former, jumping back seconds before a shiny sheet of metal sliced through the air with the merciless fury of a guillotine blade.

With his trembling body now suctioned flat against the elevator's mirrored wall, his eyes shifted back to the button at the top of the stainless steel panel. The thick black lines and curves of the number inscribed on its plastic surface blurred as he stared, scouring his brain for its significance.

His knees buckled as the elevator lurched upwards. It jerked and jarred its ascent, though not once did the shiny sheet of metal lift or slide or crack or budge. Then, suddenly plunging a freefall descent, it came to a carnival ride stop, sending him crashing into the wall.

He blinked; and when he opened his eyes, the lights had gone out. In the pitch darkness, the shrill screech of rusty gears displaced foreboding silence. The walls were closing in around him. Grinding to a halt just inches from his body, what was an elevator had become a coffin; a coffin fitted to size. He could smell the dank scent of earthworm laden soil, wafting in through cracks unseen. He could feel the satiny fabric brushing against his clammy skin. He clawed at the fabric, tearing and ripping it away. The invisible hands of claustrophobia tightened their strangulating grip. Gasping, his airway choked off, he visualized his lungs constricting, deflating, and collapsing.

He blinked; and when he opened his eyes, the walls encasing him had become transparent. Faint light shone down from high above. And with it, menacing shadows projected as jerking and twitching silhouettes onto the walls of the elevator shaft. He heard the sound of approaching footsteps, the cadence of their stride deliberately unhurried. Fixing on the steel cables, his eyes widened in panic-stricken anticipation of what was about to happen.

Anxious seconds passed before a pair of gardening shears jutted out of the darkness, the size of the glinting blades exaggerated to an impossible length. White gloved hands with invisible arms gripped their handles. He swallowed, watching helplessly as one white gloved hand waved a mocking farewell before slicing through the cables.

Bile gushed into his throat, burning it raw and trapping his terror-stricken screams as he plummeted into the shadowy abyss below.

Suddenly, he was hurled back into consciousness. He gasped, desperate and choking. His body shuddered. His eyes shot open and swept across the darkened bedroom. In the eerie stillness, even the familiar objects were tainted with a sinister air.

Slowly unclenching his sweaty fists, he glanced between the dampened handfuls of twisted fabric. His body felt weak and heavy and cold; his heart, as though he had landed on a bed of nails. He stared down at his chest, watching in fascination as it pulsated the frantic rhythm of his heartbeat.

Though the details of the nightmare were already fading, he vividly recalled a distorted shadow, trailing him through a maze of darkened corridors. The rest were impressions: fear, panic, and the nauseating sense of utter helplessness as his weakened body plunged into darkness.

Giving his head a shake, he blinked long and hard to clear the images away. Then, kicking at the mess of tangled sheets, he slowly coaxed himself out of bed.

NOW STANDING IN the crowded Métro, with his hand gripping a greasy pole, Richard Sinclair tried not to focus on the heat-stained grime of fingerprints, stamped onto its metallic sheen. The train lurched to a stop. He cringed as the doors opened to another influx of morning commuters. He gave serious consideration to calling out, '*sorry we're full,*' but for the good it would do. Then again, maybe if they thought he was crazy they would keep their distance.

Sweaty bodies pressed against him. Colognes and perfumes mingled with failing deodorants and halitosis. Gritting his teeth, he turned his face away from the head of greasy hair just inches from his nose, its musty, sweaty odor wafting up into his nostrils.

He winced as a wave of nervous rumblings began snaking through his gut, causing its contents to churn with each twist and turn. Having made it this far, he had assumed he was in the clear.

However, the consequences of that miscalculation were now being painfully realized, as was his regret at having eaten that greasy fry-up for breakfast.

"*RICHARD, YOU'RE EARLY*, come on through. Here, have a seat, I'm just finishing up."

Stepping through the front door of his Uncle Phillip's house always made Richard Sinclair feel as though he was entering into another world. Another world, in which everything was monochromatic, cold and sterile. And then there was that smell. Sniffing at the air, the familiar earthy aroma greeted his nostrils. It was the sort of faint scent that might have otherwise gone unnoticed, were it not so strikingly at odds with the austere décor. Seating himself on one of the white leather couches, he hesitated before selecting a magazine from the carefully arranged display on the glass coffee table.

Glancing down at his nephew from the landing above, Phillip Madden drew a deep breath and continued down the stairs.

"Coffee?"

Richard nodded.

Returning from the kitchen with a travel mug in each hand, Phillip looked across at him with a questioning grin. "So, are you ready to begin your first day in the real world?"

Rising to his feet, Richard set the magazine down on the coffee table, smiling to himself as he caught his uncle resisting the inclination to place it back into its proper position.

LOCATED AT THE corner of Queen and De La Commune, Blackwell Laboratories operated out of a renovated distillery building near the *Vieux-Port* in Montréal. The red brick exterior of the nineteenth century building had remained in good condition, so too had the original sash windows, their wooden frames painted dark forest green. The same red brick was left exposed on the interior walls adjacent to the entrance, capped by thick cream colored trim which butted against the glossy dark hardwood flooring. Situated between two metal staircases and propped up with shiny metallic legs, was a translucent slab which comprised the reception desk.

"Welcome abroad, Docteur Sinclair," said the receptionist,

Geneviève Dumont, her English softly spoken and heavily accented.

"It's pronounced 'aboard' dear," corrected Phillip Madden.

A slight blush dusted her freckled cheeks as her large hazel eyes moved shyly from Phillip back to Richard. To the latter, she quietly said, "I hoped with you to practice my English."

Speaking before Richard had a chance to reply, Phillip said, "*Est la paperasse dans mon bureau?*"

Despite it appearing to the contrary, Phillip's switch to French was reflexive, as though her words had reminded his tongue it wasn't supposed to be speaking English. Still, his interruption and the manner in which it was delivered, earned a critical glance from his nephew, who, resisting the urge to apologize on his uncle's behalf, simply lowered his eyes as Geneviève, with a quick shake of her head, stepped back behind her desk and handed Phillip a manila envelope.

PHILLIP MADDEN'S EXPRESSION turned serious as his eyes circled over the handful of objects arranged meticulously upon his desk. Spotting the teapot, he leaned forward and poured two cups. "It's still warm," he said, holding one out for Richard to take. Then, unlocking the top drawer of his desk, he removed a thick blue folder and placed it in front of Richard.

Glancing at the folder, Richard silently mouthed the word written on the tab in his uncle's neat hand. "*Asclepius*," he repeated aloud. "Are you writing a book?"

"That my dear nephew is the culmination of my life's work, and you are about to become the first person, other than myself to know anything about its existence."

Richard stared down at the folder, unsure of what to say.

"You are wondering why I have chosen to entrust you with this."

Richard nodded.

"Because I know in your hands my work will be protected," said Phillip, reaching for his teacup, "and, because I now find myself in need of your help."

CHAPTER TWO

Recognizing the lanky chauffeur from his previous visit, Edward Blackwell frowned his disdain. He had been easy to spot amongst the arrivals crowd, slouched against a post and looking indifferent to his task as he picked at something lodged between his teeth. He lurched upright when he noticed Edward approaching. Dismissing his attempt at pleasantries with an unwelcoming glare, Edward motioned toward his suitcase and followed him out to the car.

Half an hour later, they turned into the semi-circular driveway of Edward's childhood home in the Forest Hill neighborhood of Toronto. After helping him to the door with his suitcase, the chauffeur turned back toward the car. The suddenness of Edward's grip on his wrist sent an expression of horror to his ashen face. Meeting his startled eyes, Edward seemed amused as he reached into his pocket. Following the motion with his bulging eyes, the chauffeur released his breath when he saw the American currency. Taking a quick step back, he shook his head. "There's no need for that, sir, the old man took care of it."

Old man indeed, Edward thought to himself, reflecting on the silver haired specter that was Nicholas Turnbull, his father's personal assistant for as long as he could remember. Even when he was a child, Nicholas had given him the impression of a man well into his sixties and yet peculiarly, it seemed his appearance had never changed. It was as though he had been frozen in time at that unfortunate age, waiting for everyone else to catch up.

RICHARD SINCLAIR'S EYES moved from his uncle to the folder and back again. "Why all the secrecy?"

Phillip Madden's stomach plunged. He hated having to lie. "It's complicated, but is due in large part to a difference of opinion between my business partner and me regarding my firm belief that everyone should have equal access to the best medicine available."

"But he's your business partner, doesn't he have certain rights?"

Phillip stared into his hands. "I've had little contact with Edward Blackwell since we started this company. He leaves the day to day operations to me." Pausing, he lifted his eyes. "The truth is, he never really had any interest in the research; he was always more invested in the idea of being perceived as a scientist."

"But that doesn't really answer my question."

"Anyway, enough of this talk about Edward. I imagine you are anxious to hear more about *Asclepius* and how you fit it."

Forcing a weak smile, Richard nodded.

"I had long ago convinced myself the cure for this disease would ultimately be found in the natural world." Phillip smiled to himself as he caught the reflexive flash of skepticism pass over Richard's face. "And it was shortly after you were born that I began my pursuit in earnest. I travelled the globe, collecting samples of leaves, bark, needles, fungus... well, you get the idea." Glancing down at the folder, he paused. And as his glance lingered, shadows of contemplation clouded his keen eyes, their sharpness fading as though he was searching for some misplaced memory.

"Uncle?"

Lifting his eyes, Phillip gave his head a quick shake. "Sorry, where was I?"

"You were travelling the globe and collecting samples."

"Right, right," said Phillip, nodding. "So after having driven around for what must have been hours, we had just about given up, when suddenly they came into view like some sort of mirage. Climbing gingerly out of the parched earth, we saw the branching roots of these most strange and wondrous plants. In all of my travels I had never encountered anything resembling their peculiar morphology; they looked like enormous fungi with a tangle of spiked tentacles protruding from their caps. I preserved several clippings and upon my return home set immediately to work."

"Um, sorry to interrupt, but I think you just relayed a much abbreviated version of events. Upon your return home from where?"

"Uh? Oh, I suppose I did. Sorry Richard, my mind's all over the place. Malawi, we were there to accompany a delivery of medical supplies to one of the refugee camps."

"Who's 'we'?"

Drawing in his chin, Phillip arched his brow. "Your father never told you about the work he did over there?"

Richard shook his head.

"Huh, well, it was your father who introduced me to Dr. Jon Monteiro, the physician who helped me start up the clinic in Marsiquet."

Richard nodded. It was an absent, mechanical response. Having mentally fallen behind the pace of his uncle's words, his mind was now sprinting to get caught up. And as it did so, his thoughts streamed out of his mouth. "Wait a minute, if not here—which I am assuming to be the case, as twenty-some odd years' worth of research would be impossible to hide—then where have you been doing this work? And where have you been keeping all of the samples you collected?"

"I keep a greenhouse at home, which is also where I have conducted most of this research, save for the use of some of the analytical equipment in the lab."

Shaking his head, Richard rested his elbows on his knees and looked up at his uncle from beneath his brow. "And had I not accepted your offer to work here, would you still be telling me all this?"

"In time you will come to learn that life is a lot like the work we do in the lab, secrets are revealed in due course and often when we least expect it."

Richard rolled his eyes, his uncle's reply being the sort typical of him whenever the truth was being deliberately avoided.

"So where was I?"

"You had just returned home from Malawi."

Nodding, Phillip's tented fingers began a rhythmic patter. "It's impossible to explain why, intuition, perhaps…" As the rhythmic patter slowed to a stop, the sharpness in his eyes again faded.

Hearing Richard's discreet "Ahem," he quickly called himself back. "Regardless the underlying reason, I was certain that hidden within these Malawi specimens were the answers I had been searching for. The years that followed were spent in relative isolation, painstakingly sifting through a vast library of potential compounds, searching day and night for some indication that the progress of this disease could be halted."

"You do know all you ever had to do was ask."

"I know Richard. And it would be wrong to think it mere hubris. It was something more, something that perhaps in time you will come to understand."

"GOOD MORNING NICHOLAS," said Edward Blackwell, stepping through the opened door.

That Nicholas simply nodded in reply seemed out of character, but not without precedent. Edward's stomach tightened, recalling how the precedent had been set and subsequently reserved solely for those occasions when he had fallen out of favor with his father. Wondering if that was the reason behind this unexpected summons, he hastily scoured his memory for possible causes, but found none.

"Where is he?"

"Mr. Blackwell is in his study," said Nicholas, before turning and disappearing down the hall.

Edward set his suitcase down in the foyer and walked up the imposing oak staircase to the second floor. Continuing down the hall to his father's study, he tapped lightly on the mahogany paneled door.

"Come in."

The strained and croaking voice was almost unrecognizable. Taking a tentative step inside, Edward wrinkled his nose for the room smelled of sickness, stale air and menthol. The shutters on the windows were closed; and but for the few slivers of light showcasing the otherwise unseen particles of dust, one would have no way of differentiating night from day. In a corner of the room a large humidifier clanked and hummed.

The darkened figure behind the desk slowly rose to his feet, and when he stepped into the light, Edward shuddered. The tall metal object beside his father and upon which he now steadied himself was an IV drip. Certain that no more than twelve months had passed since his last visit, Edward recalled him having appeared in good health. And yet, there he now stood, a skeletal reflection of his former self, staring back at him through eyes that looked like watery pools of melting ice. In Edward's mind, he had already worked out the diagnosis. The word hung on his lips. Guilt melded with confusion and anger.

Swallowing back the upsurge of emotion, he approached with his hand extended, pretending not to notice either the apparatus or the sickly state of his father. Though why his instinct was not to acknowledge the obvious, he did not know. Clearing his throat, he steadied his voice. "Hello father, it is good to see you."

Thomas Blackwell eyed his extended hand, but did not take it. The effort of rising to his feet had drained him of his strength. Bracing himself between his desk and the IV stand, he groped for the arm of his chair. Edward stepped forward to help him, but a sharp and unyielding look stopped him in his place. In an instant he felt transported back in time to when he, as a boy, so eager to please and so fearing disappointment, had stood awaiting his father's judgment in this very room.

AFTER A FEW seconds of silence had passed, Phillip Madden sought out Richard Sinclair's eyes. "Your research at the university, it involved altered tumor suppressor function and its role in carcinogenesis, did it not?" Without waiting for a reply, he quickly added, "In fact, I seem to recall it having focused primarily on the role of p53. Can you tell me why you decided to focus on that protein specifically?"

His question was met with a curious expression and silence.

"Indulge me, Richard, for the purpose of this discussion."

"Because in its absence, errors that occur during cell division are left largely unchecked, as you well know."

"And as you well know, the drugs currently on the market are only effective at treating tumors in which functional p53 is synthesized, but is then blocked from acting to initiate repair."

Nodding, Richard said, "Drugs which are of no benefit in treating the other fifty percent of tumors where a functional protein is not synthesized."

"Taking that into consideration, you can imagine my

astonishment when I discovered that three of my isolated compounds were acting in concert to trigger cell death in both types of tumors."

Richard lowered his eyes.

"I know what you are thinking Richard, but this is no mere coincidence. Trust me, my controls had controls. And I resisted forming any conclusions until after I had tested these compounds on hundreds of cell lines."

"Have any shown signs of resistance?"

"None whatsoever," said Phillip, sweeping his head from side to side.

Richard was silent.

"The thing is," continued Phillip, clasping his hands beneath his chin. "Although I have determined several of the downstream pathways through which they are acting, I find myself stalled at the mechanism behind their effects on the altered p53 gene itself." Pausing, he directed his glance to the folder. "You will understand what I am referring to when you read through my notes." Lifting his eyes, he met Richard's directly. "And as such, I fear I have now reached the point where I am no longer able to view things objectively. What I need now, is for someone to help me see how all the relevant pieces fit together."

"I understand, at least I think I understand, but how exactly is this going to work?"

Phillip broke apart his clasped hands and brought them to rest upon his desk. "Take the folder home with you tonight and give it a read through. We can discuss the specifics tomorrow. I think I have given you more than enough to digest for one morning."

Staring down at the folder, a slight pensive smile bent the corners of Richard's mouth.

"What are you thinking?"

Richard tensed at the question, experience having taught him the truth of what he was thinking was always best kept to himself. His face reddened at the recollections. And yet, in the absence of speaking the truth, he was—more often than not—left with nothing to fill the void. He wondered at the source of his inability to ever manage a convincing, *'Hmm me? Oh, nothing'*. He considered attempting it now, then quickly reconsidered. The trace of vulnerability he saw lingering behind his uncle's steely gray eyes suggested this might be one instance when saying nothing proved worse than saying something, even if that something was ridiculous. "It's just that for weeks, well, in truth ever since I accepted your offer to work here, I've had this strange sense of foreboding hanging over me. It's felt like my intuition was trying to prepare me for something terrible." He paused at the sudden change in his uncles' expression. And now wishing he had opted to say nothing, he quickly added, "Not that my being entrusted with your life's work isn't reason enough for sleepless nights. But in a way, I feel as though a weight has been lifted. I don't know how to explain it, but I feel a sense of relief."

Phillip did not respond. Instead, he turned his face away and in doing so, happened to notice the message light flashing on his phone. "Sorry Richard, I better check this. I've been expecting a call from Jon." Lifting the phone to his ear, he nodded toward the manila envelope Geneviève had handed him earlier. "Standard non-disclosure forms and such, if you can just sign the first page and initial the rest."

"Right now?"

"Please, we need them for payroll," said Phillip, sliding a pen toward him.

Tucking the signed forms back into the envelope, Richard then placed the *Asclepius* folder inside his backpack, stepped out of his chair and turned to leave.

Lowering the phone from his ear, Phillip held it to his chest. "I look forward to picking this discussion up tomorrow."

Glancing back over his shoulder, Richard held his uncle's eyes, each searching the other for some clue as to what they were thinking. He then smiled, nodded and walked out the door.

CHAPTER THREE

Edward Blackwell reached an unsteady hand to his shirt collar and undid the top button. His palms were sweating. His face also bore a sheen of moisture. He blinked to control the twitches which invariably pronounced themselves in moments of extreme anxiety. Seating himself in the chair across from his father, he looked directly into his glassy eyes and saw something beyond what he had perceived as anger. Now, he was certain what he saw was disappointment. Disappointment, and a melancholy so intense it penetrated through his wasting exterior.

"Edward, I have asked you here today because I am dying," said Thomas, his gravelly voice scraping against the dryness of his throat. Lifting a glass of water to his lips, he added, "I have cancer. It is now just a matter of weeks."

Hearing the words spoken abruptly and without emotion made the croaky voice sound cruel and taunting. Edward felt his body and mind withdrawing, closing off from an inevitability he was not prepared to accept. But for the ringing in his ears and that blasted humidifier, a bleak silence filled the room. Slowly rising on weakened legs, he walked the few steps to his father's chair and folded to the floor.

Refusing him any semblance of comfort, Thomas remained still and silent as Edward wept quietly at his side.

"Okay Edward, that is quite enough. Please take your seat, there are matters we need to discuss."

Avoiding his father's eyes, Edward kept his face turned away as he rose to his feet and walked back to his chair.

Between his bony fingers Thomas held out an envelope. "I want you to have a look at this. It arrived here shortly after your last visit."

Inside the envelope was a typed letter, several pages in length. When Edward had finished reading the last page, he slammed it down on the desk. His limbs were shaking, his stomach tightening and twisting as he fought to contain the rage billowing up from its depths.

IT SO HAPPENED on this particular day, evoked perhaps by scent or sound or sight, Henry Sinclair found himself thinking back to that singular day; the one in which the course of his young life had been forever changed. It was singular, in the sense it had been the only day on personal record that he had deviated from his beeline toward the university's main doors after class. He recalled how it had been the acronym on their sign that had drawn his attention. It had never occurred to him the university would be part of the SETI program. He remembered vividly his excitement at the prospect of finding others who shared his interest in all things extraterrestrial. Hurrying off the escalator, he had threaded his way toward their booth.

By the time he had realized his mistake, it was too late to manage a polite retreat. SETA, as it turned out, stood for *Students for the Ethical Treatment of Animals*. His sense of disappointment was fleeting, however, for no sooner had his eyes glimpsed the horrendous video being played on the monitor behind their booth, than a new passion was born.

Stepping to his side, Adèle Leary had provided a whispering commentary for the video. He remembered how she had spoken with an assuredness seemingly at odds with her delicate features and slight frame.

"We meet once a week," she had said, handing him a leaflet. "Come by this Thursday if you're interested in learning more about what we do."

EDWARD BLACKWELL LIFTED his face and looked directly into his father's eyes. "Surely you cannot believe a word of that."

Silencing him with a raised hand, the delicate skin around

Thomas' naked brow arched. "You do realize they play by a different set of rules, Edward, these people you have chosen to associate with. It will take a hell of a lot more than our family name to protect you when you fall out of their favor."

"But I can explain," said Edward, his voice strained with desperation.

Again the hand rose up to command his silence. Edward stared across at him, but no longer saw him clearly. His head was spinning madly. He felt the urgent need for fresh air and yet he could not move, frozen in place as though aboard some demented carnival ride.

Resting his brow in his palm, Thomas slowly shook his head. "In a way I blame myself, I know I indulged you too much as a child."

"Please don't blame yourself father, I've never known what compels me to do these things. Something just comes over me, something I cannot control. And by the time I realize what I have done, it is too late to reverse my actions."

"It is never too late," whispered Thomas.

Edward held his eyes, hopeful. But Thomas turned away, shaking his head as his eyes traced the line of tubing extending from his fragile vein.

"No Edward. I may have been willing to accept those excuses were there just one, perhaps two indiscretions, but it is as though in your entire life, every decision, every action has been unconscionable, unscrupulous and deliberately cruel." He spat the last few words. The effort made him wheeze. Taking another sip of water, he lifted his eyes and met Edward's directly.

The trickery of light and shadow now emphasized the expression of disappointment Edward read on his father's face. The pain in his stomach was fast becoming unbearable as he fought the need to vent his rage. It was only his pride preventing its surfacing, for although his self-control was tenuous, he refused to lend any validity to the words his father had spoken.

"You have abused your privileged position and squandered your wealth on selfish ends, not once taking responsibility for your actions. Your conscience never weighed down by any sense of duty to uphold the reputation your grandfather and I worked tirelessly to build." Stretching his hand across the desk, Thomas picked up the letter and gave it a brief glance. "This is how you have chosen to spend your time. I have always given you the benefit of the doubt, refused to accept what was staring me in the face, but now it seems my worst fears have been realized." His pale dry lips curled in disgust as he let the letter fall from his hand.

Edward hung his head, unable to meet the judgmental eyes looking back at him.

"And since I have no reason to believe you are capable of making amends for a lifetime of wrongs, it is my intention to return a sense of balance to the scales."

Edward's head shot up. "But what do you mean? It is not too late. If you just have a little faith in me, I know I can be a better person. All I've ever needed was for someone to believe the good in me."

Thomas croaked a bitter laugh. "I fear it is too late for that, although, I pray for it every night."

"So you intend to cut me out, your son, and your flesh and blood? What possible purpose could that serve unless your sole intention to hurt me?"

"My intention is not to hurt you Edward, it is to make amends for your lifetime of ill-begotten deeds. It is the fate of your soul that worries me now, not your flesh and blood."

Tears of self-pity welled in Edward's eyes. For a moment he looked helpless and hurt and vulnerable; and then, slowly, his expression hardened into a look that sent a chill through Thomas' frail bones.

Lowering his head, Thomas swayed it from side to side, releasing a mournful sigh. "And now, I need you to leave."

Rising to his feet, Edward braced himself against the desk to prevent his weak and trembling limbs from faltering. His mind was in shambles. The painful lump in his throat had become so restrictive, it now felt as though air could barely pass. Treading upon unsteady legs, he made his way to the door. He did not turn back when his father called his name.

"Edward, I do hope one day you will come to understand, my love for you is my sole motivation for doing what I have done."

CHAPTER FOUR

Over a year had now passed since that singular day when Henry Sinclair had deviated from his beeline toward the main door after class. And today, as he had done so many times before, he ascended the escalator to the third floor and entered room 306.

He was the last to arrive and quickly took a seat. Those already seated had focused their attention toward the front of the room where Adèle Leary was standing. A spindly male figure, dressed head to toe in army surplus, stood behind her thumbing through a notebook.

"It's my pleasure to introduce all of you to Jack Doherty," said Adèle, casting a measured glance around the room. "We should consider ourselves fortunate to have someone with Jack's experience in the field of animal welfare on board to advise us on our activities. He was a member of the organization in the UK responsible for shutting down a number of breeding operations. Breeding operations, which had been supplying animal subjects for research testing."

To Henry's mind, Jack Doherty's resting expression seemed deliberately severe, as though he feared a smile might in some way lessen the perception of his importance. He took an immediate disliking to him. There was something calculating in his eyes, something warning, he was not to be trusted.

As Adèle continued with her introduction, Henry could feel her deliberate glances. And though he kept his eyes fixed firmly on his tightly clasped hands, he could sense her silent rebuke. No doubt she had noticed his eye shrugs, and perhaps even heard his muffled groans. Although she had not mentioned it by name, he was familiar with the group to which she had referred. He wondered how aware she was about the methods they had used to shut those breeding operations down.

Now stepping aside, Adèle motioned for Jack to come forward. Henry lifted his eyes. It was the faint Irish lilt that had drawn his attention. He had expected a harsher tone, something more in keeping with his severe expression.

"After speaking with Adèle about the direction—" Connecting with Henry's unreceptive eyes, Jack hesitated and cast Adèle a questioning glance. She nodded for him to continue. "Well, let's just say there are going to be a number of immediate changes."

Turning, Henry looked around the room, expectant of a shared sense of outrage. Instead, he was met with pulled lips and shrugs. Crossing his arms, he sat with a rigid posture, listening in defiant silence as Jack's voice rose and fell in one absurd diatribe after another. His body twitched each time he resisted the impulse to interrupt. And with his every grunt and grimace, he could feel Adèle's critical eyes boring into him. But he was too angry at that moment to care much about her opinion. To his mind, Jack Doherty was the stereotype come to life; the kind of guy who needed to be part of a cause, any cause.

He also sensed there was something unstable, even dangerous about this latest stray Adèle had taken in. And just as had been the case with her menagerie of stray felines, he could see in her eyes she was oblivious to his faults. He wondered at the exact nature of their relationship, watching as Jack rested the tips of his long, nicotine stained fingers against his boney cheek and cast Adèle another one of his questioning glances.

"About the name of the group, I've given this much thought and believe we should consider changing our name to *Fioretti di San Francesco*."

Although Jack held his thin lips tight, Henry was certain he glimpsed a gloating smirk as his eyes brushed past. Determined not to allow him the satisfaction of appearing riled, Henry sat quietly through his explanation for the name change; though beneath his composed facade, waves of indignation were twisting his insides into a tangle of painful knots.

"Do you have a problem with the name change, Henry?"

Adèle's direct address caught him off guard. And now, acutely aware of a room full of eyes fixed on him, he felt a feverish heat rising up his neck.

Swallowing, he said, "Don't you think with a name like that we're going to be confused with, oh, I don't know, missionaries perhaps?"

She replied with a grunt-headshake-eye roll combination. And having never before been on the receiving end of such a dismissive trifecta, Henry's words stalled in his throat. Unable to summon an intelligible response, he looked to Stéphane Brunot, the one person in the room, he felt certain would rise to his defense.

Set wide below a head of bright copper hair, Stéphane's warm amber eyes offered a sympathetic smile, and then quickly looked away.

Now, feeling as though the last gust of wind had just been knocked from his sails, Henry fell silent. Yielding in manner, though not in thought, his shoulders slumped forward, his eyes lowered, and his blood simmered beneath his skin.

CHAPTER FIVE

The downy clouds with their swift motion created a dizzy whirlwind of dancing leaves on the road in front of them. Richard Sinclair smiled to himself, a feeling of contentment washing over him as he breathed in their bittersweet nutmeg aroma.

"This damn thing," cursed Henry Sinclair, pounding his fist against the radio dial. "I thought you were going to get it fixed."

Richard responded with one of his arched-brow, sidelong glances; the sort which invariably made Henry feel like the crude simpleton sat next to the refined intellectual.

Turning into their driveway, they craned their necks toward the house next door, where a transport truck was blocking off access through the alleyway.

"Did you see anything?" whispered Richard.

"Nope, but surely it can't get any worse than the Browns."

"Shhhh, keep your voice down."

On the other side of the transport, a driver started honking their horn.

"Asshole, what does he expect them to do?"

"I imagine he expects them to move the truck."

Closing the car door behind him, Henry hurried across their back lawn toward the road.

Within seconds of his disappearing from Richard's view, the honking came to a stop.

"Let me guess," said Richard, catching the telling grin on

Henry's face when he returned a few minutes later. "The 'he' turned out to be a 'she'?"

They both spun around at the sound of a voice calling out from the neighboring yard.

"Thanks so much for that," she said, smiling as she caught her breath.

Realizing he was staring, Richard looked to Henry, expecting him to say something, but he too stood motionless and silent. Richard then quickly lowered his eyes, fearing his expression might look as ridiculous as his brother's.

"We knew that the truck was going to give us some grief. The movers are clearing it out as fast as they can."

Neither responded. It seemed nature was conspiring against their ability to focus on what she was saying.

"I'm sorry, I guess I should introduce myself, my name's Kate." She glanced over her shoulder toward their house. "Looks like we are going to be neighbors." Holding her smile, she searched their vacant faces for some kind of acknowledgment. And as her eyes moved from one to the other, her hand suddenly shot up to her forehead. Blinking, she started to introduce herself again, only this time more slowly and in French.

Henry's laughter startled her. She smiled through her embarrassment, but the blush lingered in her cheeks.

With an easy smile, he said, "I'm not laughing at you. Your French is perfect, but it's not necessary. It's just, well, you surprised us is all."

Meeting her eyes, Richard managed a smile, relieved to see Henry returned to his senses.

Hearing her name, she turned.

"That's my dad. I better go help." Blowing out her cheeks, she rolled her eyes. "He's in a horrible mood."

GLIDING INTO THE kitchen, Abby Sinclair hurried toward the counter to set the grocery bags down.

"Isn't it beautiful outside?" she said, directing her words to no one in particular as she crisscrossed the kitchen, opening and closing cupboard doors. Pausing by the window, she glanced outside and breathed a contented sigh. "How was your football practice, Henry?"

Looking over his sandwich, he met her eyes and shrugged.

"Well, I will need you to get that smelly gym bag out of my kitchen when you're finished eating. I've invited the new neighbors over for dinner tonight." Closing the oven door, she glanced down at the dog. "And can one of you please take Walter out for a walk so I'm not tripping over him?"

"He can do it. I need to take a shower," said Henry, jumping up from his chair.

"Thanks Richard. It looks like we may have finally gotten some normal neighbors, and I want to try and make them feel welcome."

BEN MIRONOV'S WEARY expression softened as he took hold of James Sinclair's offered hand.

"Good to meet you James. This is my wife Margot and our daughter Kate."

"Welcome, please come on through," said James, showing them to the living room. "Make yourselves at home. Abby's just finishing up in the kitchen. May I offer you something to—?"

A thud, the rumble of pounding feet and a slamming door, directed their curious eyes toward the ceiling.

"Please excuse me for a moment," said James, smiling his apology. "I better go make sure they haven't killed each other."

HER PARENTS WERE nothing like what Richard Sinclair had expected. Her father was a giant of a man with a prominent nose and large sky blue eyes. Despite his enormous size, he spoke softly and had a gentle manner. Her mother was petite and elegant with delicate, pointed features that brought to his mind her resemblance to some exotic bird.

Having yet to speak himself, Richard's eyes turned to his brother when Kate, at her mother's prompting, began to tell James about how Henry had helped them out earlier that afternoon. Although Henry's proximity to the fireplace made less obvious the reddening in his cheeks, it was his uncharacteristic silence that had drawn Richard's attention. Grinning to himself, he glanced at the source of his brother's sudden bout of modesty, quickly lowering his eyes as they connected with hers.

"THERE, I THINK that's everything," said Abby Sinclair,

placing a salad bowl down next to James. Taking a step back, she swept her eyes across the table. "You're left handed," she said, pausing at Kate, who, unsure of how to respond simply froze with her wineglass lifted to her lips. "Oh, no this won't do, you'll be bumping elbows all night. Henry, you take Richard's seat and Richard, you come over here beside Ben."

Appearing pleased with the new arrangement, Abby sat down opposite James and motioned for everyone to help themselves.

"What has brought you back to Montréal after so many years?" said James, speaking to Margot Mironov as the food made its way around the table. The question cast a sudden shade of sadness over her face and he immediately regretted having spoken so casually.

"My mother has been in the hospital here for some time, and…"

"And to make a very long story less so," said Ben, gently finishing her faltering words, "we decided it was a good time for a change of scenery."

Nodding understandingly as he reached for the dish being passed to him, James followed Ben's eyes as they moved across the table, and glimpsed what seemed to him an apologetic exchange between father and daughter; though both appearing equally contrite, it was impossible to gauge who was the injured party.

RICHARD SINCLAIR'S VIEW now impeded by the crisscrossing conversations, he tried to appear interested in what Ben Mironov was saying, but his attention kept drifting across the table. In his head, he was cursing his right-handedness, or rather his mother's annoyance with bumping elbows.

As the din of conversation slowly tapered off, his father's voice carried across the table. That he had had too much to drink was certain. Richard smiled, watching his exaggerated movements and jovial manner, so much in contrast to his usual reserve.

"I for one have always believed our canine companions are among the world's greatest opportunists." Pausing, James glanced around the table in search of some encouragement.

Kate Mironov's smile widened as she met the playful eagerness of his wine imbued eyes. "How so?"

"They know exactly what they want, and are unburdened by any sense of propriety which might otherwise hinder their pursuit." He then motioned to his side, to where Walter had been advantageously seated throughout the meal.

Glancing down at the dog, Richard grunted a laugh. "Before you go giving him too much credit dad, remember, he does lie on the same patch of grass where he urinates and is fond of eating soil from the flower pots."

Just then, the phone rang.

Springing up from her chair, Abby hurried toward the kitchen to answer it.

Returning to the dining room a few moments later, she nodded toward Richard. "It's for you."

Excusing himself, Richard walked through to the kitchen.

"I apologize for the interruption," said Abby, settling back into her chair. "Honestly, I don't know how he has managed without him all these years."

Margot Mironov's eyes widened with curiosity. "Who is this?"

"My younger brother, Richard works for him."

"He does? How interesting. What sort of work does he do?"

"Research, medical research, but I'm afraid that is all I know; both he and my brother are reluctant to ever speak about their work."

"Medical research?" Margot's thin brow arched in surprise. "But he is so young. I would have thought him near to Kate's age. My goodness, he must be very intelligent. But then again, I imagine it helps having family—" Breaking off with her lips still parted, she brushed at her flushed cheeks. "Oh my, I didn't mean to imply that being related would make him less intelligent. I just meant—" Stopping herself, she swallowed and stared down into her folded hands.

Abby's lips tightened and pulled as she considered how best to respond to what had always been, for her, a sensitive subject.

"You were right on both counts," said James, meeting Margot's eyes as they lifted at the sound of his voice. "Phillip, that's Abby's brother, he and Richard have always been close; and Richard, well, let's just say his path through school was..." hesitating, he sought Abby's eyes, unsure how much to say when the subject could return to the room at any moment.

"Accelerated," said Henry, his plainspoken tone slicing through the awkwardness with welcome precision.

RICHARD SINCLAIR COULD sense the attention of the table was focused upon him when he re-entered. It was the kind of scrutiny that made him hyper-aware of every aspect of his person. Habitual actions, programmed for decades, were forgotten in an instant: *How do I walk? Where do I look? What do I do with my hands?*

"Sorry about that," he said, meeting Margot's curious eyes as he returned to his chair.

She dismissed the need for an apology with an easy smile, though her eyes did not waiver.

He glanced at Ben Mironov, whose posture now seemed unnaturally stiff, as though he knew better than to impede her view when she had a target in her sights.

"So tell me, Richard, the research you do…" hesitating, she again lifted a delicate hand to her rosy cheek. "How thoughtless of me, you are probably not permitted to speak about the details of your research."

Lowering his chin, Richard smiled to himself. His silence was deliberate, intended to make her question her strategy. Or at the very least, to let her know that he knew one was being employed. He had not yet determined whether the immediate liking he had taken to her was because of, or despite, her liberal use of such conversational antics. Before she had decided to focus her attention on him, he had found it entertaining to watch her work the table, her acute flair for the dramatic equal to the sharp edge of her features.

"You want to hear about my research?" he said, finding it hard not to smile as he held her eager eyes.

She nodded.

"Well," he began, his eyes fixing thoughtfully on his hands as he brought them together on the table in front of him. "When certain proteins don't function properly, the likelihood of cancer developing is increased. And I've spent the past few years trying to gain a better understanding of what causes these proteins not to function properly."

"And have you?"

He lifted his eyes. "Sorry?"

"Gained a better understanding."

"My uncle seems to think so. Me, I'm not so sure."

"I imagine this type of work must be very fulfilling."

"It can be."

"Perhaps it would be a good idea for Kate to volunteer at your lab."

Kate glared at her from across the table.

"Why do you give me such a look?" Margot's manner was beyond reproach. "This is what you are studying, is it not? It would be a good experience for you to be in a laboratory environment."

"But what about the clinic?"

"The clinic is only a few hours a week. And with your schooling now delayed, I think it is best you stay—"

"If you're interested let me know," said Richard, prompted to interrupt as his eyes connected with hers.

"I am interested, but I'm afraid my mom has kind of put you on the spot."

"Not at all," he said, his nervous glance now shifting between her arm and his brother's shoulder. "In fact, I imagine my uncle will be pleased I've managed to recruit someone at no expense to him."

James erupted in a sudden coughing fit as a mouthful of wine collided with a rising tide of laughter, triggered by Richard's words. Looking across the table, his glassy eyes were met with a critical stare from Abby. Her stern expression suggesting, among other things, it might be time for him to ease off the wine.

CHAPTER SIX

Seated across from his mother at the kitchen table, Richard Sinclair could feel her eyes studying his face for signs to validate her concern. He knew that at its root, was the constant sense of guilt she inflicted upon herself for having deprived him of what she considered to be, a 'normal' adolescence. What he also knew, was that neither her guilt nor her concern could be alleviated by anything he might endeavor to say; and that his any attempt to do so, was most certain to have opposite the intended effect. And so, even though he knew that for her to be presently seated across from him, it meant she had set her alarm clock to some ridiculous hour—or not gone to sleep at all—he made no attempt to ease her worried mind.

"You're up early, do you have a busy day?"

Nodding, he kept his thoughts hidden behind his coffee cup.

"How's Kate working out?"

"She's a natural. I feel a bit guilty we're not paying her."

Abby Sinclair laughed quietly to herself. "You better not let Phillip hear you say that."

"Is there something on your mind, mom?"

"Now that you mention it, Margot was telling me Kate's birthday is this Saturday."

"Do they have any plans?"

"I don't believe so, no."

Reaching for the newspaper, she opened it to an earmarked page and pushed it toward him.

"What am I supposed to be looking at?"

She pointed to an advert at the bottom of the page. "I remember Kate had seemed quite taken with the *Sull'aria* when she heard it during dinner."

Though he had noticed as much himself, he responded to his mother's words with a blank stare.

"It might be a nice way for you to thank her for the work she's doing in the lab."

"I don't know if that's such a good idea."

"Why not?"

He shrugged.

Reaching for her purse, she removed a small white envelope and pushed it across the table. "Please don't argue with me, Richard."

As he lifted his eyes from the envelope, they were met with the portrait of maternal persuasion. It was a look he knew well, and one he knew better than to challenge—it was, at once, both gentle and unyielding.

THAT RICHARD SINCLAIR had barely seen Kate Mironov all day now only added to his apprehension as he sat in his car, in the parking lot at work, waiting for her to come down. It was a strange sensation, standing on one side of a dreaded conversation, knowing inevitably it was going to happen, but agonizing over the intervening minutes.

"Is everything okay, Richard?"

When he didn't reply, Kate turned toward her window and rolled it down. Tilting her head back, she closed her eyes and breathed in the crisp autumn air.

He tried not to notice how the sun, now low in the sky was setting her skin aglow. He tried not to breathe in the air as it teased his senses with her subtle perfume. He tried to distract himself with thoughts of work, with thoughts of anything to take his mind off his current situation.

Neither spoke for some time. It was the kind of tense silence that fills a space when two individual minds are preoccupied with thoughts of the other person.

They were stopped at a red light when, figuring it was now or never, he reached into the glove box and handed her the envelope.

"What's this?"

The light turned green.

Opening the envelope, she removed the single ticket.

He kept his gaze fixed directly ahead for fear of what jumbled mess might come out of his mouth were he to meet her eyes at that moment. "It's your birthday this weekend." His voice sounded like he had just sucked back a mouthful of helium.

"But there's only one ticket in here, unless—" She stopped herself before the words, 'you intend for me to go alone' escaped her lips.

He opened his mouth to speak, but hesitated. His mind was racing. Cringing inside, he tilted his face away. He could only imagine how foolish he looked.

"Ah, I see, so you have the other one." Laughing gently, she leaned across the armrest and kissed his cheek. "I would love to go to the opera with you this weekend."

She was now so close he could feel her words as she spoke. The impression was so strong it took a second for the sound to reach his ears. Then, as she sat back in her seat, he quietly released the breath he had not realized he'd been holding. And though he was conscious of her eyes upon him the rest of the way home, he couldn't muster the confidence to turn and meet them until after he had parked the car in his driveway.

Tilting her head back slightly, she met his eyes with an admiring smile. He focused on her voice as she spoke, but couldn't register her words. It felt as though time sort of froze or at least his awareness of it had.

And now, standing outside his car, with no sense of how he had moved through space and only a vague recollection of what had transpired in the intervening seconds, he gave her a dizzy smile before she turned and walked toward her house.

FOR A FEW minutes Richard Sinclair allowed himself to savor the contentment he was feeling. And in those brief few minutes, he felt more comfortable in his own skin than he had in a long time. But then, slowly, and without his even realizing it, the corners of his mouth downturned, as old insecurities insinuated themselves into his thoughts. Deceptive whispers in the back of his mind suggesting an alternate and less encouraging perspective on what had just transpired.

Having lost his appetite, he threw out the half eaten slice of pizza and walked through to the front room. Sitting down at the piano, he closed his eyes and attempted to drown out one kind of noise with another.

He spun around when he heard Kate's voice.

"I believe this belongs to you?" Tilting her head toward Walter, she smiled. "Sorry if I startled you. I did ring the doorbell, but no one answered... and since I knew you were home, I thought I'd just let him inside, but then I heard the piano and..."

"I hope he wasn't too much trouble."

"This guy trouble?" Bending down, she scratched behind his ear. "Nah, I think dad is warming to him."

A brief silence passed as each respective mind searched for words with which to prolong the presence of the other.

"What was that you playing just now? It sounded terribly sad. I was almost afraid to interrupt."

"I guess it is, but for some reason I've always liked it." He held her eyes for just a moment too long, before catching himself and looking away. "It's one of *Chopin's Nocturnes*, but I'm afraid I don't do it justice."

"You are too modest. I thought it sounded beautiful, sad but beautiful."

He lifted his eyes. "Do you play?"

"Unfortunately, when I was given the choice, I chose the guitar."

"Why unfortunately?"

Smiling, her head fell gently to the side. "I only chose it because I wanted to be the cool one with the guitar around the campfire at parties."

"And how did that work out for you?"

"Not so good."

Finding herself at a loss for something more to say, she turned and walked slowly around the room, pausing every few steps to look through the books on the bookshelf, the family photos, and the CD's in the rack.

Dusk had fallen and was casting its blue-gray hue across the room. In the fading light, she seemed to him some ethereal creature; the creation of an idyllic daydream, that might at any moment vanish as quickly as it had been conjured. And as his thoughts continued to drift, he imagined what it would be like waking up next to her. He pictured himself staring into her eyes, dark blue like the ocean. He imagined tracing his fingertips over her smooth skin, illuminated by the glow of the early morning light, and her golden hair falling loose around her shoulders, and...

"Richard?"

Her soft voice struck him with a guilty jolt as a flush crossed his cheeks. He blinked, shook his head and attempted to mask the truth behind a serious smile. "Sorry, what was that?"

"I asked if I could hear you play something else before I go."

"What would you like to hear me play?"

"Perhaps something a little more uplifting."

"Hmm, I'm afraid I don't really do uplifting. How about you give it a try?"

A nervous smile passed her lips as she sat down beside him. "Is this where you teach me to play chopsticks?"

"Don't look so worried, *Mozart* actually intended this piece for beginners."

"Oh, okay, so it's just a little *Mozart*, should be a piece of cake."

He gestured toward her hand; and as she placed it in his, he felt it tremble slightly. "Just relax and let my hand guide yours."

Although the warmth of her body next to his was a welcome distraction, he was nonetheless relieved to have chosen a piece he knew by heart. Seeing her genuine amusement as her bright eyes eagerly followed the rapid movement of their hands across the keys, was, for him, the witnessing of a reaction he had not known himself capable of bringing about. But then, as swiftly as it had begun, the piece came to a sudden end, leaving him wishing he had made a different selection.

Turning her hand over in his, he smiled admiringly. "I knew it, you're a natural."

Gently drawing her hand back, she lowered her eyes.

When they lifted, he felt saddened to see that their brightness was fading. He was at a complete loss to explain the sudden change in her expression. All he knew was how the change made him feel. And to see the brightness fading from her eyes felt like watching storm clouds move across the sun.

"What is it?" He spoke softly.

She was silent.

He sensed her eyes were pleading with him to do something, but what? And what if the 'what' he was thinking was wrong, and he did it anyway, and made a complete fool of himself? At that moment, he desperately wanted to be the kind of guy who didn't hesitate and over-think, the kind of guy who knew on instinct what to do.

She drew back at the sound of Abby's voice. It was as though in an instant she had closed herself off completely, like some beautiful flower with its petals drawn in tightly.

"I better go," she said, edging off the bench.

He reached out his hand, but she did not take it. "Kate, if I've done something to upset you I—"

"You haven't done anything wrong. I'm just feeling emotional. It must have been the music." She forced a weak smile, but could not bring herself to meet his eyes before turning and hurrying out the door.

CHAPTER SEVEN

Jack Doherty slowed the car as they neared VNP Laboratories. In the seat beside him, Adèle Leary sat nervously chewing on her thumbnail. From the back seat, Henry Sinclair regarded her anxious profile, wondering again how it was she had managed to convince him to go along with their plan.

The front of the building, with its clean lines and mirrored facade was a stark contrast to what they saw as the car approached the back. Enclosed by twelve foot high fencing topped with barbed wire, it more closely resembled a high security penitentiary than a clinical testing facility. Henry felt his stomach churning and heard it rumble and wondered if it was too late to back out.

Parking on an unlit side street, Jack got out and opened the trunk. Henry shuddered when it closed, sealing him and Adèle inside. Topping his list of worst fears, was the nightmarish visualization of being buried alive. His pulse raced as a rush of tormenting thoughts swirled around his head. They were the sort of irrational thoughts that brought into question whether Jack might indeed be capable of such an act.

Stopping at the security gate, Jack held out the identification card. After giving it a quick glance, the guard handed it back and waved him through. Proceeding forward slowly through the massive metal gates, Jack turned right and drove toward the east entrance of the building. Parking in a darkened section of the lot, he got out and opened the trunk.

Henry and Adèle found the fire exit door had been left propped open, just as Jack had told them it would be. Exchanging an uneasy glance, they drew their breath and stepped inside. Once through the door, they descended a flight of stairs, and continued down the length of a dimly lit corridor. At the end of the corridor, Jack stood waiting for them in front of a large freight elevator. Anxious seconds passed before the doors finally opened.

Inserting the key card into the bottom of the digital panel, Jack entered B3 into the keypad. The elevator began to descend.

GLANCING UP FROM the reservation book, the hostess forced her plump red lips into a plastic smile as she led Richard Sinclair and Kate Mironov to a corner table, tucked away from the other patrons. It was a slightly shorter version of the hostess, who then returned with the wine and took their orders.

They each attempted to fill the silence that followed with helpings of bread and sips of wine. He had seen little of her since the other day when she had behaved so strangely. And in the car they had barely spoken, but at least there the radio had taken some of the edge off. Swallowing back another large sip of wine, he scoured his mind, searching for something to move them past their conversational impasse.

"Are your parents settling in alright?" He watched as she picked up a stray crumb of bread and placed it onto her side plate.

Without lifting her eyes, she quietly said, "Mom and I both love it here, but I think dad is struggling a bit. The move was a big change for him. He has lived in San Francisco all of his life."

"He sounded alright when he was at our house."

"That's just his way. He only agreed to move here because he felt it was in the best interest for mom and me."

"I'm sorry, yes, your grandmother. Are you two close?"

"Not particularly."

"Then, why for you?"

"Huh?"

"You said the move was for your mom and you."

She met his eyes with a guarded smile. "Did I?"

Nodding, he followed her eyes as they broke away and lifted toward the waitress, who was just then arriving with their food.

"*WHATEVER HAPPENS, JUST* stick to the plan," whispered Jack Doherty, his icy blue eyes focusing intently on Adèle through the holes in his mask.

Henry, having caught the split-second it took for Adèle's anxious eyes to harden, breathed a shaky breath; grasping, in that moment, the potential consequences of what Jack had said about a drop in temperature triggering the refrigeration unit's alarm system.

She swiped the key card over the scanner. Hearing the mechanism unlock, Jack pulled the handle down and towards him, opening the door just enough for him and Henry to wedge their way through.

Despite the freezing temperature, Henry could feel the beads of sweat trickling down his back. Turning on his flashlight, he was suddenly confronted with the macabre sights on display before him. Staggering back, he blinked hard, thinking his nerves had caused some sort of visual distortion.

Jack handed him a camera. "Be quick."

Darting around the massive freezer like a startled mouse, Henry's trembling hands could barely hold the camera steady for long enough to photograph the deformed and mutilated specimens on the shelves.

A few minutes later, Jack stepped to his side and placed a hand on his shoulder. Henry drew back in fright, nearly dropping the camera. Pointing to his watch, Jack motioned it was time to leave.

"*IT'S OKAY, KATE,* I've never been the guy people feel comfortable opening up to."

Kate Mironov paused with the fork held midway to her mouth and set it down. Richard's stomach knotted as his words replayed in his head. Lowering his eyes, he chided himself, knowing she would now think him either pathetic or manipulative—or both. Still, he could not deny her evasive manner had piqued his curiosity.

"You should probably consider yourself lucky."

Lifting his eyes, he caught a glimpse of one of her vaguely flirtatious smiles just before it faded from her lips. And feeling a peculiar sense of relief from her response, he lifted a few small forkfuls of food to his mouth in rapid succession, less from hunger than to prevent his saying anything else absurd.

Her expression grew animated as she finished her last bite. "Now it's your turn."

"My turn?"

"Yes, now you must tell me something interesting about yourself."

Though relieved her somber mood seemed to be lifting, he wondered if he had missed some subtle cue, some faint indication of how it had suddenly become his turn.

"Girlfriends?" Her candor brought a slight blush to her cheeks.

Catching this, and feeling somewhat emboldened by it, he held her eyes and slowly smiled. "A few, but nothing serious."

"Hmm," she murmured, lowering her eyes. Her head suddenly felt light. She could feel the intensity of his eyes upon her and when she lifted hers, she knew at once the source of her light-headedness. Tightening her lips, she attempted an air of mild impatience, but doubted she was succeeding.

Emptying his wine glass, he deliberated a moment longer. "Well," he said, brushing past her eyes as he set the glass down on the table, "I wouldn't really call it interesting, but I'm afraid it's all I've got."

"Go on," she said softly, tempering her eagerness.

"When I was in elementary school…" he hesitated; hearing his words play out in his head suddenly made what he was about to say sound very much the opposite of interesting.

"Did something awful happen?" Her tone was cautious, as though half fearing the answer.

Smiling, he shook his head. "No, no, nothing traumatic. It's just I got moved ahead a few grades." Pausing, his eyes flickered thoughtfully. "Actually, now that I think about it, perhaps it was slightly more than a few."

"Oh, that." Her relief was audible as she exhaled through her words. "Your parents had mentioned something about that at dinner."

"But I was there. When would they have had—" Suddenly recalling their only opportunity, he tightened his lips and shook his head.

"Don't be angry. It wasn't their fault. Mom has a way of getting information out of people. Dad says it's what makes her a good lawyer."

Nodding, he smiled.

"Still, being so young, it must have been difficult for you to—"

They both turned toward the waitress, who, looking between them, held Richard's eyes for a moment before reaching across to remove their plates.

"What was all that about?"

"All what?"

"That look you gave her?"

"I don't know what you are talking about."

Returning, the waitress set their coffee cups down on the table. And then, with a pleasant smile, which now appeared genuine, she removed a dish of crème brûlée from the tray and set it down in front of Kate.

"How did you know this was my favorite?"

"I asked your mother."

"You did? But when?"

"Make a wish."

Closing her eyes, she blew out the tiny flame. "Thank you, Richard. I mean it. This was really thoughtful."

"It is my pleasure." Reaching his hand across to remove the candle, he caught sight of his watch. A look of panic crossed his face. Craning his neck to get the waitress' attention, he motioned for the bill.

SITTING ON THE edge of the sidewalk, with his head in his hands, Henry Sinclair watched Jack and Adèle through his fingers as they spoke in hushed tones beside the car. Focusing on their lips, he tried to make out what they were saying. They each had lit cigarettes in their hands, though neither seemed to be paying them much attention, their tense fingers anxiously flicking the dangling lengths of ash.

Now holding her cigarette in the air, with her free hand bracing her elbow, Adèle looked on as Jack paced the sidewalk in an escalating state of agitation. He came to an abrupt stop at Henry's side. "Now do you believe me?"

Blowing out his cheeks, Henry ran his hands down his face. "What the hell was that place?"

Jack held his eyes a moment before sitting down next to him. "Have you ever heard of a guy called Edward Blackwell?"

Henry opened his mouth to reply, but unable to gauge where this was going, he hesitated.

"It's okay, Henry, you don't need to answer that, we already know about his connection to your family."

Henry's muscles tensed. He could feel Jack studying his face for a reaction.

"Well, what you just saw in there was a glimpse inside his demented mind."

Glancing over his shoulder, Henry wondered how much of this Adèle had already known about when she was convincing him to come along.

"Maybe now you can begin to understand why I have committed my life to exposing monsters like him," continued Jack, his voice now low and stripped of its usual impassioned tone.

Henry stared down at the pavement, his mind unable to move past one question in particular out of the many, now queuing in his head. "I saw the dates on the tags. Some of them were from two years ago. Why wouldn't they have incinerated them? Why keep them in that freezer?"

"It's a well-known fact that psychopaths like to keep trophies."

Henry grunted. It was a non-answer, the kind suggested in the absence of any rational explanation. "What are you going to do with the photos?"

"We'll hang on to them for now."

"For now?" He watched as Jack reached into his pocket and lit another cigarette.

Blowing the smoke away from Henry's face, he gave him a sidelong glance. "I've been gathering information on Edward Blackwell for some time now, and if we have any hope of exposing him, we need to be smart about it. Trust me, he's as slippery as he is demented."

Henry held his eyes with an unvoiced question.

Jack nodded. "Tonight wasn't the first time I've seen something like this. I've seen examples of this kind of torture at every research company he's involved with."

"There is no way my—"

"Your uncle's lab is an exception. But that's only because

Edward has been barred from stepping foot in there."

Henry attempted to conceal what he was thinking as the words 'barred from stepping foot in there,' repeated in his head, but judging from the look on Jack's face he wasn't succeeding very well.

Leaning in close, Jack lowered his voice. "It's like I said, I've been researching this guy for some time."

Henry was silent.

"It's only natural you would want to discuss this with your family, but for the time being we need to keep this strictly between the three of us. Others knowing would jeopardize everything I've been working toward."

Henry looked him squarely in the eye, but didn't speak.

"Don't worry Henry, we know we can trust you. Otherwise, we wouldn't have brought you along with us tonight."

"Trust is a two-way street remember."

"Fair enough," said Jack, tossing his cigarette on the road as he moved to stand up. "And now I need to get this car back before they notice it's missing."

"Wait a minute, whose car is that?"

Jack smirked. "Whose do you think? The plates had to match the ID. We're just lucky I happened to bear a striking resemblance to some bloke called Larry Curtis."

"You mean we've been driving around in a stolen car?"

"Don't worry about it."

"But what if it's been reported stolen?"

"Relax, it's all been taken care of."

PARKING IN THE underground at *Place des Arts*, they quickly made their way through the corridors and up the stairs, arriving at their seats just as the lights were dimming.

Under the veil of darkness, what were at first discreet glances, gradually became less so. And although Richard Sinclair felt an almost intrusive observer, capturing the intimate moment when one form of beauty is drawn to another, he could not bring himself to look away. He marveled at the nuances of Kate Mironov's expressions, shades of emotions he had not known it possible to convey.

Every so often she would tilt her head back or to the side,

accentuating the contours of her neck and the angles of her face, completely oblivious to the effect her every movement was having on him.

He regarded the very rhythm of her breathing in humble fascination, watching as she closed her eyes and breathed in deep, almost sensual breaths, her chest trembling ever so slightly with each release.

In the final moments of the last act, all he could think about was how he didn't want the night to end.

CHAPTER EIGHT

Kate Mironov was to Richard Sinclair's mind the most intriguing puzzle nature had ever placed in his path. Though she could read his every insecurity, she did not—like others with this similar ability—seek to use it to her advantage; instead, she sought to rid him of them entirely.

Though he acknowledged that the scars of personal experience had led him to bestow upon her qualities of an embellished nature. It was those very same scars that would have had him mired in feelings of inadequacy, were it not for the fact that such superficialities didn't exist in her world. It was as though she hadn't been given the societal rule book on how girls who looked like her were supposed to conduct themselves.

One day, and in a roundabout way, he managed to steer the conversation toward this topic. And when he asked her for her thoughts, she spoke of how when she was little, she used to stand on her tiptoes and trace the different colored threads of an embroidery that hung on the wall beside her mother's dressing table. She said she had memorized the embroidered words, but had not fully understood their meaning until she no longer needed to stand on her tiptoes to trace the threads.

As was her peculiar habit, she said no more, contented to leave it there. She had often told stories in that way, starting or finishing at some random point and then leaving him to fill in the gaps.

"What did it say?"

"Hmm?"

"The embroidery, what did it say?"

"*Beauty can only be regarded for so long before you have its measure and grow tired of looking at it.*'"

She then lowered her eyes and fixed them back on the menu in her hands. The subtle action, her not so subtle way of making it clear she had nothing more to say on the subject. And he knew better than to try pursuing it any further. He had willingly accepted this and her many other eccentricities as part of what made her so interesting.

And yet, as autumn's breeze gave way to winter's chill, he found himself needing to know more, needing to know everything about her. Replacing all others, she had become his first thought in the morning, his last before drifting off to sleep. And with each passing day, she slowly began to reveal to him the various nuances of her personality. Soon, he was able to anticipate her moods and when necessary, conduct himself accordingly. Recognizing how when she was in an especially good mood, she would stop at nothing to ensure everyone around her was equally happy. And how when she was upset, it was best to leave her alone until the mood had passed. And how, when he was in her presence, the insecurities that had plagued him for as long as he could remember, seemed to vanish into the ether.

CHAPTER NINE

Unlike his brother, Richard Sinclair's mood had been more in keeping with the somber atmosphere of the cold and dreary day. Driving along a monotonous stretch of flat and open highway as they headed back to Montréal, it seemed winter's monochromatic hues were doing little to alter his current frame of mind.

Exhausting all other mental distractions, Richard's thoughts now yielded to work; more specifically, to the assays he had run before leaving the lab on Friday. The same discrepancy that had been nagging at him for months, had shown up again in the results. And this time, having controlled for every conceivable variable, he was now left with only one explanation for what he was seeing. In and of itself, this was encouraging, and would have been welcomed as progress, but for the fact that the explanation he was left with was impossible. He searched for an alternative. He searched for something he might have missed. His head felt like a heavy bag of sand, through which he was sifting for a singular grain. His foot fell heavy on the gas pedal. He needed to get back to the lab.

They were about an hour outside Montréal when Henry Sinclair awoke. Night had fallen. The sky was crisp and dark with bright points of light piercing through its charcoal veneer. For a few minutes he regarded Richard's tense profile unnoticed.

"You know you're a workaholic, right?"

Richard gave him a quick sidelong glance.

"You're going to end up like Uncle Phillip if you're not careful."

"What do you mean by that?"

"I mean alone, unable to relax and married to your work."

"How can you say that? We had a good time in Boston, didn't we?"

"Yeah, yeah this weekend was fun. But if I'm wrong, then tell me what you were thinking about just now? And don't even bother trying to lie because I know you too well."

Richard was silent.

"Yeah, I thought so."

"Sorry Henry, I guess some things are just hard-wired into my nature, whether I like it or not."

"You know those *Patriot's* tickets were like gold, eh? I still don't know how Kate managed to get them. We are going to have to get something very nice to thank her."

"I know; and we will."

Richard endured his brother's silent and sulky demeanor for the remainder of the drive, unable to pretend the pangs of guilt over his two day absence from work weren't twisting his stomach into a tight knot of anxiety.

ARRIVING AT THE lab later that same evening, Richard Sinclair was relieved to find the building empty. Relishing the idea of working uninterrupted, he walked with hurried steps down to the basement.

Alone now, and with Kate miles away, it struck him how for the first time in his life he had been finding it near impossible to concentrate on his work. The persistent distraction of thoughts of her had so often made him resentful of the late hours spent alone in this room.

Drawing in a deep breath, he began reading through the data he had collected over the past few months. For some time his eyes moved between the images of sequencing and protein gels taped to the pages of his notebook; and then to the assay results printed in the tables below. The hours passed slowly.

Turning off the desk lamp, he closed his eyes and leaned back in the chair. In the darkness, he tried to close off his mind to all distractions and focus in on what he was missing. At first, the images crossed his mindscape like slow moving frames of film, pausing briefly as he considered each through to its likely conclusion. Gradually, the images began to cycle by faster and faster; and then, right at the point when his head was spinning and he felt he was going to be sick, the truth revealed itself, like a blinding flash of light. He bolted upright in his chair. His eyes wide. His mind alert.

Reaching across the desk, he turned the lamp back on. He then quickly flipped through the pages of his notebook, searching for what he had previously overlooked: the data that would validate the impossible. Picking up the phone, he dialed his uncle's number. After five rings a groggy voice mumbled something resembling 'hello' into the phone. In his excitement, Richard spoke quickly.

"Richard is that you, it's..."

Richard listened as he fumbled with something on the other end.

"It's 3:00 a.m. Can this not wait until I come into the office?"

"Sorry, Uncle, I didn't think to check the time before I called."

"It's okay Richard. We will talk soon. Please, just try to get some sleep."

His mind still reeling, Richard slumped back in the chair with a contented smile on his face. After a few minutes, he got up and walked over to the closet and removed his sleeping bag. Throwing it over himself, he turned off the light and was asleep in minutes.

CHAPTER TEN

Phillip Madden's imposing frame cast a shadow over Richard Sinclair's closed eyelids. Smiling down at him as they suddenly shot open, he handed him a cup of coffee.

"What time is it?"

"6:00 a.m."

"Is anyone else in yet?"

Phillip shook his head.

"Do you remember anything I said last night?"

"I don't think I registered anything beyond your announcing you had found something."

"Please sit," said Richard, pushing out the chair he had been resting his legs on. "My head is pounding and it's far too early to be speaking above a whisper."

Handing him a bottle of tablets from his pocket, Phillip seated himself in the offered chair.

Washing two back with a large mouthful of coffee, Richard stared down into his cup as he spoke. "It seemed impossible. So impossible, I managed to convince myself there had to be another explanation; one that meshed with everything I know to be true."

Listening attentively, Phillip sat with one arm resting on the back of the chair, the other on his lap.

"I was looking in the wrong place. The whole time it was there, right in front of me, but until last night I didn't see it." Richard lifted his eyes. "I am now certain that your three compounds, by acting either directly or indirectly are triggering a cascade of repair reactions in such a way as runs contrary to accepted principles."

Phillip was about to speak, but hesitated. Leaning forward, he clasped his hands beneath his chin, and nodded for Richard to continue.

"I am talking about the recognition and meticulous correction of errors within the primary RNA transcript of p53. Corrections, which then in turn, lead to the translation of a functional protein. It is, in essence, a reversing of the consequences of mutations within the gene itself."

Phillip was silent. With his chin still resting upon his clasped hands, he stared down at the floor. Richard studied his expression for some clue as to what he was thinking. He blinked when the large clasped hands suddenly fell to his lap. He then watched through wearily expectant eyes as his uncle stepped out of the chair.

"There's something I need you to do for me."

"The 'how', I know; I'm already on it. Last night I was thinking I would... What? Why are you giving me that look?"

"You didn't let me finish. I was about to say, what I now need you to do, is to go home and get some quality sleep." He held Richard's eyes until certain his words would be heeded. Then, slowly turning, he walked toward the door. "Go home Richard. Go home and get some rest."

CHAPTER ELEVEN

Landing squarely on the bridge of his nose, the cold and wet chunks of plaster jolted Richard Sinclair awake. Wiping his face with the back of his hand, he narrowed his eyes and followed the trail of water trickling down from the ceiling and along the window frame. Dodging a second showering of plaster, he rolled out of bed and hurried downstairs to the kitchen.

"There's a leak in my ceiling."

Slowly turning, James gave him an unenthusiastic glance.

"Sorry dad, but it's pretty bad."

Breathing a heavy sigh, James stepped out of his chair. "Alright, I'll go and have a look."

Richard walked over to the patio door. "It sure is a mess out there."

Without turning, Henry nodded. "They're saying the accumulation of ice is causing the hydro towers to collapse."

Following his brother's eyes to the images on the television screen, Richard ran an uneasy hand across his brow. Turning back to the patio door, he slid it open and poked his head outside. The color drained from his face.

Abby was ready with a reassuring smile when she met his eyes. "They probably decided to pull off somewhere for the night."

"If they did, it's going to be a while before they can get back home," said Henry, motioning toward the television. "They've closed off access to the city over concerns about the weight of the ice on the bridges and tunnels."

"How the hell did they miss this?" Richard's raised tone was accusatory as he looked between them. "What's the point of having meteorologists if they can't even forecast something like this?"

They turned when James walked back into the kitchen.

"How does it look?"

"He was right Abby, it's pretty bad. The ice must be damming up the eavestrough. And until this storm passes we won't be able to get anyone in to repair it." Pouring himself a cup of coffee, he turned toward the television. "Let's just hope they can keep the hydro flowing into the city. I don't know how the hospitals will cope if they all lose power at the same time."

"I'm sure they're doing everything they can to prevent that from happening."

"Still, I think it is best if I head in before this storm worsens."

"And just how do you plan on getting down there James? You can't drive and they've shut down the Métro."

STEPPING OUTSIDE, IT was as though they were entering into some surreal snow globe landscape. The scenery was both breathtaking and unsettling. Everything was sheathed in a thick crystalline veneer of ice, frozen in place as it had been at the precise moment the initial storm had struck.

The singular interruption to the eerie silence that filled the empty city streets was the even more unsettling crack and crash of tree branches, snapping off and falling to the ground. It was the kind of silence and emptiness that seems especially strange in an otherwise bustling city. Though in Richard Sinclair's anxious state, the scene felt more zombie apocalypse than New Year's Day; it was the sort of silence and emptiness that had him compulsively glancing over his shoulder while scouting for weapons of convenience.

Blustering bursts of freezing rain pelted them from all sides as they walked in silence, each with their eyes fixed calculatingly on the sidewalk below.

Drawing back when his father placed a hand on his arm, Richard followed his eyes up toward the glazed over street sign.

"I guess this is where we part company. Remember to call your mother when you get to the lab."

"I will," said Richard, stepping down into the intersection.

His ice-covered boots cautiously gripped the surface of the glassy sidewalk as he continued south along Peel. Having nearly lost his footing several times already, he began to wonder how long it would take for someone to find him, were he to slip on the ice and crack his head.

"RICHARD YOU LOOK awful. Get out of those wet clothes. Wait here, while I get you something warm to drink."

Returning a few minutes later, Phillip Madden handed him a steaming cup of coffee. "Is Abby okay?"

Cradling the warmth of the cup between his frozen hands, Richard nodded. "You had mentioned on the phone there was something you wanted to discuss."

"Yes, yes, I did," said Phillip, resting his folded hands upon his desk. "How would you feel about accompanying me on my next trip to Marsiquet?"

"When were you planning on leaving?"

"As soon as this storm lets up and they reopen the airport."

"How long are you going for?"

"It will be a short visit, a week at the most."

"And you're okay with both of us being away from the office at the same time?"

"I will take the necessary precautions on my end. Just be sure to bring everything related to *Asclepius* home with you before we leave."

"You still think Dr. Toreli suspects something?"

Phillip arched his brow. "Think?"

"But I've been so careful, only ever working at night when I'm absolutely certain no one else is here. And the drugs, the files, I bring everything home with me when I leave."

"I know Richard, I know. I am afraid as long as Edward is pulling his strings, he is not to be trusted."

Richard was silent.

"Just let that be a lesson to you, never give anyone, least of all a man like Edward Blackwell, the opportunity to hold something over your head." Reclining back in his chair, he met Richard's eyes with a heartening smile. "I really think you would benefit from the experience. And meeting Jon, well, that is reason enough for you to come along. He is an extraordinary man, and was instrumental in helping me get the clinic up and running. Oh, it's a modest operation mind, but it is some comfort to know the children in the surrounding villages are receiving vaccinations they would otherwise not have access to."

Richard's expression softened. "I'm sure I can manage a week away."

"I am very pleased to hear that, Richard. And I will arrange for someone to assist with your work while you're away. Speaking of which, I imagine we will now be seeing a bit less of Kate's beautiful face around here."

"Unfortunately, this storm has delayed her start."

"What? You mean they've closed the university?"

Richard nodded.

"The airport I understood, what with the runways and all, but the university? I had no idea it was that bad."

"Haven't you been watching the news?"

Phillip's features twisted into an expression of distaste. "I had to turn it off. Too many opinions and not enough reporting."

"Fair enough, but you might want to make an exception when your city is in the midst of a natural disaster. Which reminds me, I better go and freeze down my cells, just in case."

"I don't think that is necessary Richard."

"Are you certain the generator will cover us if the power goes out?"

"I am absolutely certain."

Slowly rising to his feet, Richard started toward the door. "You know where to find me," he said, glancing back as he slung his wet clothes over his shoulder.

"Place them on the radiator in the lab and they should be dry by the time you leave."

CHAPTER TWELVE

Hesitating in the entryway to the living room, Abby Sinclair watched nervously as James warmed his frozen hands by the fire. Stepping to his side, her hand trembled as she set the glass of brandy down on the wooden mantel.

"Are the boy's home?" He spoke without turning.

"Yes, they're upstairs. James, what's going on? You said you had bad news." The words poured out of her mouth in a single anxious breath.

"I need to get the boys."

Emptying the glass, he walked out to the staircase and in a strained voice, made almost unrecognizable in its hoarseness, called out for them to come down.

He was standing in front of the fireplace with his back turned when Henry and Richard came in. Noticing the tears welling in their mother's eyes, they exchanged a worried glance and sat down beside her on the couch.

Staring into the fire, James swallowed against the tightening in his throat. Gathering his strength, he tried to steady his voice. "I was working in emergency when the ambulances brought them in." Hearing Abby gasp, the words he had yet to speak collided with emotions he could not bring himself to turn and face directly. "I'm afraid there's been a terrible accident."

His senses numb to the intensity of the pain, Richard felt nothing but a dark and cold emptiness as the world closed off around him. His vision tunneled, making everything seem distant, blurred and fading. He was not conscious of his mother's heaving shoulders or how tightly her hand was holding his own. Deflecting the images of thoughts too painful to bear, he focused upon a singularly sought version of reality, as though through the force of his denial, he might somehow be able to reverse the hands of time. Closing his eyes, he pleaded for a merciful reprieve from time, from an inevitability he was not prepared to accept.

CHAPTER THIRTEEN

All at once, the swollen gray clouds in the darkened sky ruptured, releasing a deluge of freezing rain. Coarse ice pellets slammed against their car with unrelenting fury, instantly coating windows, mirrors and wipers in an icy sheath.

Easing his foot off the gas, Ben Mironov shot Margot an anxious glance. She met his eyes with a smile of reassurance, quickly turning away before he noticed the truth concealed behind her forced expression.

Now barely moving, Ben inched the car along the highway, doing the little he could to avoid a collision. Kate's muscles tensed at the blurred images of cars spinning out around them in a nightmarish silhouette.

Agonizing minutes passed before an exit ramp finally came into view. Slowly guiding the car onto the ramp, Ben was relieved to see no headlights following behind them. And with the immediate fears of being rear-ended or sideswiped now removed, he relaxed his tense limbs, sensing the worst was behind them.

On the eastbound express lane of the highway from which they had just exited, a transport truck, laden with a heavy load, was suddenly forced to veer around the barricade of stopped traffic. Swerving across four lanes, it came careening down the icy ramp.

Everything went dark.

For some time the reprieve of dreamy blackness protected Kate from the unimaginable pain of her reality. But its merciful refuge was suddenly shattered by the glare of flashing lights and sirens.

And through the chaos and the pain she was able to read the expressions on the faces of the paramedics standing over her. And as she did, an agony with which no physical pain could ever compare overwhelmed her. She tried to scream but could manage no sound. She tried to move, but her limbs would not obey her command. She consciously resisted their efforts to resuscitate her, clawing her way deeper into the darkness and away from the light. Already buried deep within the domain of her subconscious were the excruciating memories of what had transpired before the paramedics arrived. It was as though within her, some protective force had instinctively acted to suppress them. And as she closed her eyes and blocked out the light and retreated into the darkness, those memories remained hidden in the inaccessible recesses of her mind, never to rise to the surface.

CHAPTER FOURTEEN

Abby Sinclair's stomach churned as she paced the hallway outside Kate Mironov's hospital room. She looked over to where Henry and Richard were seated. Her heart sank further. Turning away, she bit down hard on her trembling lip, fending off the urge to rush across and take them in her arms.

They looked up when the doctor approached. After he exchanged a few quiet words with Abby, she turned to Richard and nodded.

MEETING KATE MIRONOV'S eyes, the emptiness inside Richard Sinclair suddenly felt like a heap of leaden sorrow. He froze. It was as though her fragility and despair had created an invisible barrier preventing him from moving toward her.

He had passed hours outside her hospital room, trying to put himself in her place so as to know what to say when this moment finally came, but each time, he had found it impossible to truly identify with the magnitude of her loss.

Seating himself on the chair beside her bed, he gently reached for her hand and held it to his cheek. Though she lowered her eyes, he could hear her shallow and rapid breath as she fought to hold back her tears.

"I thought I'd lost you… I don't know what I would have done if…"

Slowly lifting her watery eyes, she conveyed a depth of emotion that choked his words in his throat. He rested her hand at her side, but could not bring himself to let go. Neither spoke for some time as they held one another's eyes, articulating in silence the emotions which could not be expressed in words.

"I feel guilty for not wanting to leave, but..." he hesitated at the tightening of her grip on his hand. "But visiting hours are almost up and mom and Henry are still waiting outside to see you."

"You will come back?" Her whispered voice was raw and strained.

"Tonight." Leaning forward, he gently kissed her forehead. "Is there anything you need me to pick up for you?"

She inclined her head toward an overnight bag on the floor. "The nurse told me your dad dropped it off. Please thank him for me."

"I will," he said, rising from the chair.

With his hand on the door, he paused and glanced back, moved by the sudden need to reassure himself she was really there.

CHAPTER FIFTEEN

Although Richard Sinclair knew the expectation of frigid wintry air rushing into his lungs was irrational, it made the effect of receiving the opposite all the more intense. Stepping outside *Maputo International Airport*, the stifling humidity instantly stirred up unpleasant childhood memories of trips to greenhouses with his mother: Of him and Henry, standing and sweating uncomfortably as she piled trays of annuals into their little arms.

Having fallen behind his uncle's brisk stride, Richard now watched as his hand shot up and waved in the direction of a blue jeep, idling with its hazards on. Gripping the handle of his suitcase with his sweat-glazed palm, Richard quickened his pace to catch up.

Dr. Jon Monteiro stood well over six feet with a thin frame, glistening bald head and a round face with soft, empathetic features. He eagerly took hold of Phillip Madden's hand and welcomed him with a warm smile. Then, as he regarded Richard's appearance, his expression turned sympathetic. It was the sort of sympathetic look that made Richard instantly aware his efforts to conceal his discomfort were failing. Managing a polite smile, he watched as Jon stepped back, folded his arms and nodded with a smile of recognition.

"Ah, I see it now. The resemblance is slight, but I can definitely tell you are relations." Jon considered him a moment longer; then, turning back to Phillip added, "A younger, handsomer version of you, perhaps."

At hearing the seldom produced sound of his uncle's gravelly laugh, Richard glanced over at him with a curious smile.

"Jon, this is my nephew Richard, James' son, remember I told you he is now working for me at the lab."

"Yes, I seem to recall you having mentioned it once or twice," said Jon, his warm amber eyes casting a wink in Richard's direction.

Narrowing his own against the bright sun, Richard held his smile, resisting the urge to wipe away the beads of sweat collecting along his upper lip.

"*EVERYTHING ALRIGHT AT* the clinic, Jon?"

Although Dr. Jon Monteiro had known this conversation was inevitable, his body tensed at hearing the words which would now force him to broach it. Gripping the steering wheel, he gave Phillip Madden a reluctant sidelong glance.

Recognizing the look at once, Phillip prepared himself for the receipt of bad news.

"Phillip, it struck without warning. We had barely begun to recover from the damage caused by that horrific cyclone. I was at a complete loss to help them."

Phillip drew a quick breath. A shudder ran through his entire body, leaving tensed muscles quivering in its wake. Against reflex, he held his tongue—the need to ask why he was only hearing about this now, obviated by their decades of shared experience. And guided by an intuition, borne of those same shared experiences, he steadied his voice and said simply: "How did it present?"

The alteration in Dr. Jon Monteiro's demeanor was faint, but even so, the change was what Phillip had intended by asking that question over another, perhaps more sympathetic.

"It presented with a high-grade fever, chest and abdominal pain and fitful dry cough. Within eight to twelve hours, there was hemorrhaging in the upper respiratory tract, with few victims surviving beyond twenty-four hours from the onset of symptoms. In addition to the extensive pulmonary tissue damage, post-mortems also showed lesions in the gastrointestinal tract and marked necrosis in the bladder and kidneys." Pausing, he released what little remained of the breath through which he had just spoken. And with his clinician's air of detachment quickly fading, he cast Phillip a disheartened glance. "There was simply no time to respond."

"Have you been able to identify the pathogen?"

"*Mycobacterium bovis.*"

"*M. bovis?* You mean they had tuberculosis? But how is that possible?"

"I have sent tissue biopsies and sputum samples out to a private laboratory in the UK for further testing. But until I know more, I have to rely on the information I am receiving from the hospital's pathologist."

"Which is what, exactly?"

"We are dealing with a fast-growing, hyper-virulent strain of *M. bovis*; and one which is exhibiting multi-drug resistance *in vitro*." Pausing, he breathed a heavy sigh. "And therein lies the paradox."

"Paradox?"

"I would have expected something this aggressive to be highly contagious, and yet, that does not appear to be the case."

"Asymptomatic?"

"Tuberculin skin tests were negative. The Ministry had a team out collecting blood and sputum samples from those who had contact with the victims, but we are still awaiting the results."

"And the livestock?"

"Also tested negative."

"But if it's a strain of *M. bovis*, it must have originated—" Stopping himself mid-thought, Phillip quickly changed his question. "Okay, so going back to your contagion paradox, have you been able to establish any kind of pattern?"

"The negative tuberculin skin tests have removed the possibility of an asymptomatic 'patient zero', as well as any threat of carriers harboring the bacteria. The results have also ruled out person to person transmission via aerosol and bodily fluids. Which leaves us with a scenario involving some manner of direct contact with the pathogen's source. That said, I have not been able to identify a single common factor unique to those who became infected. It's as though they each pricked their fingers on the same infected needle, and now that needle has been buried within an immense haystack."

"And the Ministry? From what you said, it sounds as though they have been quick to respond."

"Initially, yes; though in the absence of any new cases, well, you know how these things work." Pausing, he glanced at Phillip. "The problem is, without their assistance, I simply lack the resources to conduct a proper investigation myself. And in the absence of a proper investigation, how am I supposed to prevent my patients from uncovering that buried needle again?"

CLOSING THE FRONT door behind him, Henry Sinclair stepped out onto the sill and looked between them.

"Are you going to invite us in or what? It's freezing out here," said Jack Doherty, shuffling impatiently on the front step.

Henry's eyes narrowed as they met Adèle Leary's directly.

"Is there somewhere we can talk in private, Henry?"

"Right now?"

She nodded.

Grumbling his reluctance, Henry reached his arm behind him and opened the front door. They took their time removing their boots and carefully placing their coats over the others on the coat rack. Glancing over his shoulder toward the kitchen, Henry motioned for them to hurry, his preference being to avoid a forced introduction to his mother.

Adèle stopped just outside his bedroom door. "Can I use your washroom?"

"It's just down the hall, first door on the right."

Standing with his arms crossed, Henry watched as Jack sat down at his desk and swept his eyes around the room, surveying its contents with a thin, appraising smirk.

"So what's this all about? It's not like the two of you to drop by for a social visit."

Jack laughed. "Sorry to disappoint, but this is not a social call."

They both turned when Adèle entered the room.

"Did you find it okay?"

"Huh?"

"The washroom."

"Oh, yes, I found it, thanks."

Jack jumped to his feet. "You know what? Perhaps now is not a good time."

Henry looked at Adèle and could see at once there was guilt lurking behind her dark eyes. "Will one of you please tell me what the hell is going on?"

"Relax Henry. We were just talking about an idea I had, well, arguing more like, and when Adèle realized we were in your neighborhood, she suggested we run it by you. But now that we're here, it all seems quite silly to be honest."

Without another word, they turned and hurried out of his room and down the stairs. Barely pausing in the foyer, they shoved their feet in their boots, grabbed their coats and rushed out the front door.

THE CLINIC SEEMED to Richard Sinclair a peculiar oasis, perched as it was, the only visible structure of any kind for as far as the eye could see. In appearance, it reminded him of the portable out-buildings from elementary school. The ones which, if he remembered correctly, were always freezing in the winter and stifling in the summer.

Dr. Jon Monteiro stopped briefly at the side of the building to unlock the generator, before leading them up the wooden steps to the front door. Immediately beyond the door was a small waiting area, where conjoined plastic chairs were positioned opposite a large bulletin board, displaying health brochures and notices. Three doors branched off a short corridor. One of the rooms was Jon's office and the other two were examination rooms.

The children, with their innocent expressions and curious eyes, were much more interested in Richard's presence than that of his uncle. And it was due in no small part to that interest, or rather to silly faces he was making back at them, that not one child cried when Jon administered the vaccinations. Not only were tears avoided, but each time Richard sucked in his cheeks and stuck out his tongue like a lizard; and most especially, when he blew up his cheeks with an invisible pump, they were replaced by bouts of bubbly giggles.

Though as the day wore on, it gradually came to be that even the bubbliest of bubbly giggles was no longer enough to counter the effects of sweltering heat and jet lag. Richard's complexion was growing increasingly pallid, damp clumps of hair were clinging to his sweaty brow, and it was becoming harder and harder for him to keep his eyelids apart.

At one point, he blinked one of those prolonged blinks, the kind from which you startle yourself alert. And when his lids shot open, his attention was immediately drawn across the hall to Jon's office; to where a large map, marked-off with different colored thumbtacks, was hanging on the wall. And in that instant, although his outward appearance remained unchanged, his mind was suddenly awoken by an idea.

Meeting Jon's eyes during a pause between patients, Phillip discreetly tilted his head in Richard's direction.

"You've done well to last as long as you have," said Jon, offering Richard a sympathetic smile. Then, directing his glance toward Phillip, he added with a chuckle, "If I remember correctly, your uncle did not fare quite so well on his first trip. Go out and get some fresh air. I shouldn't be too much longer."

"PERHAPS YOU WILL feel better if you tell me what is on your mind."

Richard Sinclair's eyes slowly lifted from where they had been fixed upon an island of crabgrass amid the sea of parched earth, outside the clinic. "It's about the conversation you and Jon were having on the drive down here; and how he had said he was lacking the resources to conduct a proper investigation."

"Go on."

"For something like what he described to have happened, it has to have left a footprint. And being as it's so isolated out here, it's possible that footprint has not yet been disturbed. So what I was thinking was, if Jon could arrange for a translator, I should have enough time to conduct at least a preliminary investigation over the course of the next two days."

"I feared you might be steering yourself in that direction." Pausing, Phillip raised his eyes to the sky and breathed a heavy sigh. "Your mother would kill me if she knew about any of this. Hell, if I had known in advance, I wouldn't have brought you along."

"Didn't I hear Jon say there hadn't been any new cases in over a week?"

"Be that as it may, there are still certain risks involved in what you are proposing. And considering our time constraints, it does seem highly ambitious, even for you."

"I can't explain why I feel so strongly about this, uncle. All I know is when I saw the map on the wall in Jon's office, it triggered something. Straight away I knew, if only I could see all the pieces laid out in front of me, the source of the outbreak would become clear."

With his hands clasped in front of a non-committal smile, Phillip held his nephew's eyes for a short time before speaking. "You have not yet told me what you think about the clinic."

"Haven't I? Well, I think the work you and Jon are doing here is truly inspiring."

"Thank you, Richard, somehow I knew you would understand better than anyone else."

CHAPTER SIXTEEN

Towering over Oscar Ribeiro's slight five foot frame, Richard Sinclair shook his offered hand and thanked him for agreeing to help. He found something instantly compelling in the symmetry of Oscar's features. His eyes were the shade of espresso, set wide and deep above a rosebud nose and full mouth, lending him an air that was at once unassuming and precocious.

"I am pleased to help," said Oscar Ribeiro, his voice the low-toned and hesitant cadence of one self-conscious about speaking an unpracticed tongue.

That aside, Richard could not read the slightest sign of reluctance in his demeanor. Considering the circumstances, he wondered what Jon could have possibly said to convince him to come along. What words could have persuaded him to place his confidence in someone he had never met? Someone with an idea that had taken shape in the span of five minutes, while staring at a map on a clinic wall.

"You should probably get going," said Phillip Madden, glancing up from his watch; the lines of worry on his face now more pronounced with words becoming reality.

Nodding, Jon's expression was grave as he looked between them. "*Vá com Deus*," he said, handing Richard the backpack of supplies. "You have a difficult day ahead of you."

STRETCHING ACROSS A clearing of rusty earth were some thirty round-walled huts of varying size, each topped with a conical thatched roof. On the eastern edge of the settlement was a sparse pasture, whereupon Richard Sinclair could just make out a couple of cows and a few goats and sheep lying beneath the shade of the trees.

"Are you ready?"

Through a slight tightening in his stomach, Richard managed a firm nod. Though as they proceeded down the slope and everything suddenly became very real, he wondered if he would have had the courage to proceed, if not spurred on by the confidence his companion had so readily placed in him.

Entering the settlement, they immediately caught the attention of three men seated beneath the shade of a thatched overhang. With some assistance from the two younger men, the third, a man well into his sixties, rose out of his chair and approached. His dark features set into a hardened expression as he listened to Oscar explain the reason for their visit. He then narrowed his cloudy eyes and studied Oscar carefully before speaking his reply.

Richard followed their conversation closely, straining to hear any words he might recognize so as to get some sense of how his intentions were being received. He watched as Oscar reached into his pocket for the note Jon had written to accompany them; and was relieved to see a slight softening in the lines around the elderly man's eyes as they moved back and forth down the piece of notepaper.

Passing the note back to Oscar, he then slowly turned and extended an arthritic hand out to Richard. "Joseph Borrego," he said, his voice low and grainy.

Richard accepted his hand gently and introduced himself in a similar quiet manner. Having committed Jon's patient files to memory, he immediately recognized the surname: *Anna Borrego, aged fifty-two.*

"You are brave to come here so soon after what has happened," continued Joseph, fixing Richard with the same studied look he had given Oscar moments prior.

Although his English was weighted with a low, guttural inflection, his words were spoken with such unanticipated fluency, it took Richard a moment to register their implication. Uncertain of how to respond, he lowered his eyes and stood silent as his thoughts flashed back to the promise he had made to his uncle.

And as he pictured the face mask, tucked away inside his backpack of supplies, he knew there was no way he would feel comfortable putting it on in front of this man. He followed Joseph's gaze as it moved toward the somber faces of those who had begun to gather. His thoughts drifted to home, to Kate. It was impossible for him to be in the presence of such sadness and loss and not be reminded of what she must be going through.

"Wait here," said Joseph.

Standing with slouched posture, Richard kicked at some loose stones on the ground. He lifted his eyes when Oscar gently tugged on his sleeve. Joseph was motioning them over to a seating area, where four wooden benches were arranged beneath a large bamboo canopy.

Now seated, and with his notes organized on the bench beside him, Richard looked across at Joseph and arched his brow.

Joseph nodded for him to proceed.

"In the days preceding the onset of the illness is it possible Anna may have come into contact with anyone outside the settlement, say at the market perhaps?"

Joseph's expression was grave as he closed his eyes to call back memories. He was silent for some time.

Glancing to his side, Richard exchanged a look with Oscar; both now wondering if asking Joseph and the others to relive their ordeal was going to prove too much for them to bear.

Slowly, Joseph's lids drew apart, laying bare the sad traces of his recollections. "No," he replied, his voice barely above a whisper.

Lifting the pen from his notebook, Richard waited until Joseph, with a slight nod, conveyed he was ready to continue. "Is it possible she may have consumed milk or meat from a source other than your own livestock?"

Shaking his head in reply, Joseph's eyes followed the jerking movement of Richard's hand as it jotted down a few quick notes in an illegible language of abbreviations and symbols.

"Would she have had any direct contact with the other victims before she began showing symptoms?"

"It is possible, yes. Some who had worked with her tending the crops also became ill around the same time." Breathing a heavy sigh, he shook his head. "The people here, they believe that is where the sickness came from, the earth, the soil. For weeks now, it has been only my son, Abel, who will go out there."

Richard circled both Anna's name and 'soil' and placed a question mark between the two words. "And when the symptoms began—the fever and the cough—was anyone other than you in direct contact with her?"

Joseph tilted his head toward where, amongst the others who had gathered, the two young men whose attention they had drawn upon arriving were now standing.

Richard looked out into, and then beyond the small crowd. "And your water?"

"You will find the well over there," said Joseph, his curled fingers motioning to the east.

Glancing up from the page as he wrote, Richard said, "Can you recall if Anna had altered her routine in any way in the days preceding the onset of the illness?"

Staring into the hollows of his cupped hands, Joseph said, "Several days before she became ill, she went to Yaibel to soak her hands in the hot spring." Gently shaking his head, his dry lips pressed into lamenting smile. "She spent too many years tending to the crops; it left her with terrible aches in her hands."

"Did she go on her own?"

Again, Joseph tilted his head toward the two young men.

Reaching into his backpack, Richard retrieved a map and spread it open on the bench beside him. "Joseph, can you indicate where the hot spring is located?"

"It is around here," he said, pointing to the map. "Though it is now more mud than a hot spring."

"Earthquakes," said Oscar, answering the unvoiced question on Richard's face.

Marking off the area, Richard set his pen down in the spine of his notebook and refolded the map. "I apologize for putting you through this Joseph, but the answers to how this illness originated might be hidden in the smallest of details, the seemingly mundane things we do each day without even realizing it."

Stretching his arm across the table, Joseph placed his hand on Richard's and pressed it lightly. A question lingered behind the melancholy in his eyes. It was as though part of him was still trying to work out the motivation behind Richard's presence. After a few seconds, he gently drew back his hand. "We are finished?"

Richard nodded.

Turning, Joseph looked out into the faces of those who had gathered. The sound of Oscar's voice drew his attention back.

"Richard, I can continue here if you want to start collecting the samples."

"I will stay with him," said Joseph, reading the hesitation on Richard's face. He then motioned forward the older of his two sons. They exchanged a few words before both turned to Richard. "My son Abel will go with you. He knows little English, but I have explained to him what it is you need."

ARRIVING HOME FROM class, Adèle Leary followed the stinking trail of stale cigarettes toward the kitchen. The pungent tang of burnt coffee lent a bitter taste to the dense haze of noxious odors filling the small room. The sinking in her stomach sent its visceral warning. Buying time to organize her thoughts, she emptied the ashtray into the trash bin and turned off the coffee pot.

Although aware of her presence, Jack did not lift his eyes from what he was doing. Spread in disarray across the kitchen table were rolls of duct tape, a pocket knife, firecrackers and stacks of photocopied notes.

Seating herself in the chair across from him, Adèle watched as his long fingers sifted through the gray powder with easy dexterity. He then poured it into a hollowed tube and inserted a fuse. She spoke. Whether or not he had heard her voice over the music, he responded neither in voice nor manner.

Standing up in an abrupt huff, she walked over to the counter and turned the radio off. This got his attention. Tilting his head, he gave her a hard, questioning stare.

"You want to tell me what's going on here, Jack?"

Holding the tube between his fingers, he flashed a wolfish grin. "This is our insurance."

Panic filled her eyes as they fixed on the fuse, dangling from one end like some rodent's tail.

"Don't worry Adèle. It's not like these can cause any serious damage."

"But they won't know that."

"That's the point, luv. They are only meant to serve as a

distraction; smoke and mirrors, remember?"

THERE WAS A bitterness in Abel Borrego's expression that warned any conveyance of sympathy would be presuming a degree of familiarity beyond what was welcome. And so in silence, Richard Sinclair followed as Abel led him eastward along a heavily-trodden path.

Arriving at the well, Richard remained a few steps back while Abel loosened the ropes, lowered the bucket, and reeled it back up. With a nod, Abel then silently motioned for him to come forward and collect his samples.

The livestock showed little interest in their presence — save for one curious goat—but they all looked to be in good health. After filling several collection tubes with earth, pellets and stools, Richard labelled each as best as he could and placed them into the cooler with the others. They then continued along the path in silence.

The crops weren't showing any obvious signs of neglect. Though to Richard's mind, the task Abel had undertaken, seemed a responsibility far beyond the capabilities of any one person. He wondered what could have possibly motivated someone so young—someone who had just lost their mother—to put themselves at risk with neither gloves nor mask to protect them. While in the midst of that thought, he noticed several lengths of green piping, stretching up a barely perceptible incline toward a creek. After organizing the soil samples next to the others in the cooler, he made a few quick notes, and then motioned to Abel that he was going over to the creek.

Standing at the water's edge, Richard watched for some time before working up the courage to follow Abel's example. Setting his reservations aside, he crouched down and dipped his sweaty hands into the cool water, splashing it over his neck and arms. The irony of his actions was not lost on him as he then proceeded to stretch his arm down and collect his samples.

It was a long walk out to where the latrines had been built. Given the parched state of his throat and his introspective mood, Richard welcomed the silence. Despite his having watched as Abel cupped his hands and drank the water from the creek, he could not bring himself to do the same. Whether Abel had read anything into that or even regarded it at all was impossible to know, and he had near given up trying to gauge the mindset of his silent companion.

Breathing in the toxic stench of raw sewage left to fester in the sweltering heat, Richard fought hard against the involuntary urge to retch. Dodging the buzzing iridescent flies, whirling around the hole in the center of the concrete slab, he crouched down beside it. Then, gripping the collection tube by its rounded bottom, he lowered his hand, just grazing the surface of the sludge with his arm fully extended. He kept the tube submerged for a second longer before lifting it to the surface. Then, jumping to his feet, he pushed through the door and vaulted outside with a shudder, gasping to fill his lungs with fresh air.

At first, the crack in Abel's stony expression was faint, a barely perceptible smirk. But then, as his eyes locked onto Richard's sludge covered hand, he could no longer control the surge of pent up emotion. He bent over, clutching at the pain of unused muscles as he struggled to catch his breath through snorts of laughter.

Had he not needed to repeat the process, Richard might have been more inclined to see the humor in his appearance. As things were, however, his demeanor remained grim as he slid on a fresh pair of gloves and walked back toward the latrines.

Glancing up from his backpack after placing the last sample in the cooler, Richard was disappointed to see that Abel's handsome features had set back into their hardened and bitter expression. They walked back along the footpath in silence. Several times Richard parted his lips to speak, but each time his intuition advised against it. He began to think about how very different his life was from Abel's. It was difficult for him to imagine a life in which every day meant having to walk such distances for the essentials; and then, having to share them with an entire community. Thinking about that word, and what it really meant, the idea of community; it was an awakening. It brought to his mind how he could count the members of his family on one hand; and how, until Kate had moved in next door, he had made a deliberate effort to avoid his neighbors. He wondered why that was. Was it simply because in his life, necessity didn't drive the formation of such relationships? And in the absence of necessity, he had little interest in learning about those who occupied the space around him. He considered how his own city had just been brought to a grinding halt when the electricity had stopped flowing; and how the loss of that necessity had changed people, in a good way, at least for the most part.

Tilting his head back, he glanced up at the sky. In the wake of the setting sun it appeared marbled as shades of blue swirled around brilliant crimsons and tangerines. It now felt as though the heat was radiating up from the ground more so than down from the sky. He wondered how Oscar had managed with the interviews, and thought about how fortunate he was to have had his help.

THEY BARELY SPOKE during the drive back to the clinic. Richard Sinclair was relieved to find Oscar Ribeiro wasn't the sort who felt compelled to fill empty space with tedious chatter. It was one of a growing list of qualities he admired about him. Suddenly aware he was staring, Richard quickly turned his face away. He hoped Oscar had been too tired to take any notice. Although whether he had, or had not, or even given it a second thought, the effect on Richard was the same. That is to say, it served as a reminder of what it was he had always found so bothersome about meeting new people: certain understandings just couldn't be taken for granted.

As dusk fell, its dreamy twilight was doing little to entice his eyes to remain open. Soon his lids were drooping like dew soaked petals. Drawing his tongue over his parched lips, he could taste the dried salt and dreamt of the long cool shower, he would take as soon as he returned to the hotel. Resting his head against the window, he soon fell into a state of mental numbness. A barrage of complex emotions were vying for his attention, but he held them at bay; his mind was too exhausted for any serious contemplation.

CHAPTER SEVENTEEN

His fatigued body having proved an unworthy opponent for his restless mind, Richard Sinclair awoke from a slumber throughout which only his eyes had received any actual benefit. He moved to sit up, but both mind and body felt mired in a tangle of cobwebs. Slowly stretching his stiff and aching limbs, he relaxed his tense muscles and sprawled out limp atop the bed sheets like a starfish out of water. Closing his eyes, he focused on his breathing, and tried to free himself from the gauzy impediment. Several more minutes passed before he finally attempted to rise out of bed.

STEPPING OUT OF Oscar Ribeiro's car, Richard Sinclair followed the largest in a network of fissures threading through the tawny earth toward what now remained of the hot spring in Yaibel. Standing at the edge of the large oblong and muddy trench, he slid his backpack off his shoulder and removed a few collection tubes. Then, crouching down, he stretched out his arm and proceeded to collect samples from the murky basin.

He listened as Oscar spoke of how the landscape had at one time appeared, and of the many trips he had made there with his grandmother when he was a child. Though in truth, he was having a hard time reconciling Oscar's nostalgic descriptions with the desolate scene now sprawled out before him. His current deficiency of imagination brought back memories of Rome; specifically, of him standing next to his mother looking out at the *Forum*, wondering at her ability to reanimate the ruins in her mind when all he could see was a toppled heap of stones.

A massive shadow suddenly blanketed the landscape in darkness. Tilting their heads toward the sky, they watched as heavy gray-bellied clouds glided swiftly across the sun. With his head still tilted, Oscar breathed in the air.

"It smells like rain. We better go before the wind decides to change direction."

"WHAT THE HELL was that we just passed?"

Pulling off the road, Oscar Ribeiro reversed along the gravel shoulder. "It's a feedlot; you know, where the cattle are fattened up before slaughter."

"It seems strange Jon wouldn't have mentioned this in his notes."

"Why strange?"

"Remember what I was saying yesterday, about *M. bovis* typically being spread to humans from infected livestock."

"Yes, I remember. You called it a zoonotic disease."

"Right, well, given the size of that operation and its proximity to the settlement, it seems a possibility worth considering."

"You are unlikely to find what you are looking for in there."

"Why do you say that?"

"They have strict Biosecurity measures in effect. They don't even permit their workers to leave the site." Oscar pointed to a large rectangular structure to the east of the feedlot. "They house them over there."

"But the cattle, are they sold locally?"

"They are for export, to Europe I think. I have never been inside, only seen the invoices."

"Invoices?"

"They buy feed supplements from the company I work for."

"What kind of supplements?"

"You know, vitamins and minerals, the kind that make the cattle grow large and not get sick."

"Huh, that's a little unsettling."

"Why unsettling?"

"I guess I've never really given it much thought, but we eat what they eat, right?"

"I don't think you need to worry about that. By the time they reach the slaughterhouse, whatever they have consumed at the feedlot would have already passed through their system."

Keeping his thoughts to himself for fear of causing offense, Richard Sinclair put a physical end to the subject by reaching down into his backpack for his notebook. "Where were you headed before we stopped?"

"My work." Oscar pulled back onto the road. "You will see the building when we turn the next corner. I thought you might want to collect some samples."

"Samples of what?"

"During manufacture, waste flows out into a reservoir at the back of the building. The grates are only supposed to be opened at night, after the waste has been treated. But I know for a fact that many times the operators forget to close them."

Richard's eyes widened. Unfolding the map, he approximated their current position and traced the arteries of waterways leading back toward the settlement.

"But if you're right," he said, glancing up from the map, "are you not afraid someone might see you?"

"Of course. That is why you will be collecting the samples."

"But what if someone sees me?"

"There is no need for you to worry, the guards are not armed."

A shiver passed over Richard's skin as the imposing gray structure came into view. Even in a landscape of juxtapositions so peculiar they bordered on the surreal, did the cold and institutional architecture of this building seem out of place.

Parking behind a dense covering of brushwood, Oscar pointed to a section of the barbed fence beneath which the ground had been eroded.

Without giving pause for thought, Richard grabbed a handful of collection tubes from his backpack and opened the car door.

"Just be quick," said Oscar, indicating toward a depression in the brush that marked the path for him to take.

Crouching low, Richard hurried along the path and ducked beneath the opening in the fence. Not daring to lift his eyes, he knelt at the reservoir's edge and quickly filled the tubes with the sludgy liquid. Then, screwing on the caps with a turn of his trembling thumb, he stuffed them into the pockets of his jeans, and made an adrenaline fueled dash back to the car. With an audible shudder, he crashed down hard in the seat next to Oscar.

Smiling to himself, Oscar tucked the sports section back behind the visor. "I wouldn't have thought you could move that fast."

With shaking limbs and pounding heart, Richard gasped, "Let's... just... get... the... hell... out... of... here."

LOOKING THROUGH DR. Jon Monteiro's notes, Richard Sinclair read his written words aloud:

> "'Maria Tregeira, aged sixty-eight, was the last reported case of the variant M. bovis infection. To my knowledge, she was the only victim to have resided off the settlement and had no obvious connection to the other victims. Tuberculin skin tests on the family were negative.'"

A slight young man approached as they were getting out of the car. Bridging the brow between his dark, almond-shaped eyes, was a deep-set furrow; the effect of which was to set his angular features into an angry, though strangely poetic expression. And as Oscar explained their intentions, the dark almond-shaped eyes remained fixed not on him, but on Richard.

For his part, Richard read more guarded curiosity than outright hostility in his cross-armed, chin-jutting manner. And with a stoicism borne of extreme fatigue and acquired empathy, he withstood the scrutiny, unflinching. That was, until another shadow passed over the landscape. At which point he lifted his eyes toward the dark and heavy storm clouds above and silently pleaded with them to hold out, just a little bit longer.

The young man nodded and grunted his side of the conversation, his eyes unwavering until Oscar held Jon's note out for him to take. Reading it over, he responded with another grunt and handed it back. Signaling his approval to Richard with a near imperceptible nod, he then turned and motioned for Oscar to follow as he headed back up the path toward the house.

CHAPTER EIGHTEEN

It was without conscious effort that during the short drive to the airport, Richard Sinclair began dismantling the barriers he had deliberately erected upon leaving Montréal. He closed his heavy eyelids. Then, slowly, as though through pinholes of light, her image began to permeate his thoughts. And before long, the reflection of her face was all he could see.

"I am going to have to leave you here," said Dr. Jon Monteiro, removing their suitcases from the back of the jeep. "I need to get these samples over to the customs office."

"I will keep you updated on my progress."

"That would be most appreciated Richard. I only wish I could see that brain of yours in action for myself. From what Phillip has told me, the process is something truly extraordinary to witness."

IT HAD BEEN dark when their flight departed the previous Sunday and it was only now, as the plane began its descent that the extent of the storm ravaged landscape came fully into view. Huge swaths of forested area had been destroyed, brought down by the weight of the ice on their branches. Richard Sinclair's eyes traced the succession of collapsed transmission towers and downed power lines.

The scene of devastation was so surreal, it leant to his still groggy mind the absurd impression that in their absence, some invading force of metallic giants had been defeated. Their disgraced and mangled corpses now heaped masses of crumpled metal, lying splayed across the snow covered landscape.

FRIGID AIR GREETED them when they exited the airport in Montréal. Though strangely, Richard Sinclair did not so much as grimace at the bitter-cold reception. And stranger still, he was finding himself filled with the vague impression he had never really left. At first, he figured the familiarity of the surroundings was behind his hastened acclimatization. But then, as they walked in silence toward the parking lot, he considered an alternative explanation. Attributing it instead, to his mind's grappling with the stark juxtaposition of where he had been and where he was now. Catching his uncle's curious glance when they reached his car, he smiled lightly, putting the matter to rest as he passed him his suitcase.

During the drive home from the airport, Richard's mind travelled back to the place he had just left with such lucidity that when he opened his eyes, it took him a moment to regain his bearings. And now, with his head resting against the window and his eyes following the familiar transitions of the snow-covered landscape, he slowly began to realize it was going to be far more difficult to leave the world he had just left behind than it had ever been to enter it.

SETTING HIS SUITCASE down inside the door, Richard Sinclair breathed in the warm and familiar scents of home. The kitchen was dim, lit only by the faint light streaming in from the dining room. Noticing the empty casserole dishes on the counter, he figured they must all still be next door. Thinking it strange Walter had neither barked nor come to greet him, he breathed a heavy sigh and walked out toward the dining room, certain he was about to find him nose-deep in something he had managed to pilfer from the counter.

The scene with which he was met could not have been more different than what he had anticipated. Drawing a quick breath, he stopped in his tracks as six despondent faces lifted and fixed their collective gaze upon him. A colossal sense of melancholy hung like a cloud over the table. His instinct was to offer an apology for having missed the funeral, but his words were stalled by the thought of cutting through the silence with his voice. Instead, he froze, looking down, unsure of what to do.

Rising from her chair, Abby Sinclair met him where he stood and wrapped her arms around him. "Richard love, I didn't hear you come in." Taking a step back, she held him at arm's length and looked him up and down. Concern took the place of the sadness in her eyes. "You look like you have not slept in days.... You have lost weight.... Did he not feed you?"

Looking past her, he glanced toward Kate. His heart sank. She looked like an angel trapped in purgatory. By way of an apology, he quietly said, "We did try to get an earlier flight, but there were delays at *Heathrow*."

His father's eyes were ready with a look of understanding. Henry just looked desperate to escape. There was a brief silence before Abby thought to make the introductions.

"Richard, this is Kate's brother Kevin and his wife Veronica."

As his mother spoke their names, Richard responded to each with a slight nod, their guarded expressions warning against the inclination to extend his hand. He couldn't find the slightest trace of family resemblance in Kevin's features. Rather, his protruding blue eyes and gaunt appearance bore a more striking likeness to the anatomical skeletons from science class. And Veronica, he found her resemblance to a Siamese cat so uncanny, he could envision her undergoing a transmutation at any moment and scurrying out the door. He blinked the images away.

Acutely aware of Kevin's bulbous eyes fixed critically upon him, he attempted to convey in his demeanor the proper balance of solemnity and affability; this, while rummaging around his jet-lagged brain for something appropriate to say. Growing more certain by the minute that his presence in the room was having the opposite of its intended effect, he was relieved when no one raised any objections to his request to be excused.

RETURNING TO THE dining room after a long hot shower, Richard Sinclair felt a slight sense of relief to see the others had left. Joining his family at the table, he reached for the bottle of wine and poured himself a glass. "I'm really sorry I couldn't be here to help out this week, and especially today."

"Don't be too hard on yourself. Once Morticia and Gomez arrived, they kind of took over."

"Henry, you really shouldn't refer to them like that," said Abby, her weary voice lacking in any real conviction.

"What? That's what Kate calls them. I don't think they take it as an insult."

"How is she doing?"

Abby's warm features offered him their gentle reassurance. "Honey, this is the kind of wound only time can heal."

"How was your trip?" said Henry, his tone both overt and unapologetic in its appeal to change the subject.

Staring into his wine glass, Richard took a moment to consider his words before answering. "It was inspiring," he said, thoughtfully.

James gave Abby a nostalgic smile. "Do you remember when Phillip was trying to get that whole project up and running?" he said, his expression softening with the recollection.

Sharing his smile, Abby nodded. "I had never seen him so energized."

"I imagine you must all be exhausted. Why don't you go on to bed, I can clean this up."

"Just leave it for the morning, Richard." Covering a yawn with the back of her hand, Abby slowly rose to her feet.

Stepping to her side, James tenderly placed his arm around her. "Perhaps it is best if we leave the catching up for tomorrow as well. I am curious to hear what your impressions were. It's been years since I was over there."

STARTLED BY THE sound of Kate Mironov's whispering voice, Richard Sinclair searched through the darkness for some confirmation he had not just imagined it.

"Don't worry, it's safe for you to come over, Morticia and Gomez have gone to bed."

Hearing his laugh brought a smile to her face.

He crossed over to her porch. "What are you doing out here? The cold can't be good for your arm."

"I just needed some time alone to clear my head."

He took a step back.

"No, no, I didn't mean you. Please, come and sit with me."

"Are you sure?"

"I'm sure."

"Just give me a minute to get Walter back inside."

"THIS IS ACTUALLY a pretty nice set up," said Richard Sinclair, catching the glow of a heat lamp as he sat down beside Kate Mironov.

Holding his eyes with a wistful smile, she reached down for the blanket and pulled it over her arm. "I've been spending a lot of time out here lately."

"Kate, I am really sorry I couldn't be here for you today."

"You're here now."

"And the service, it was…?" He hesitated, unsure of how to finish his question. Nothing sounded right in his head. *It was good? What you wanted? What they would have wanted?*

"It was strange being in a church."

He waited a few seconds for her to say more and when she didn't, he voiced a gentle prompt: "Strange?"

"All I could think about was the time mom tried to take us to church when we were kids and Kevin ran screaming down the aisle, straight out the front door."

He started to laugh, then stopped himself. "What scared him?"

"He never said, but I think it was the statues."

"You weren't scared?"

She tilted her face toward the starry night sky. "I think I was more curious than anything."

In the silence that followed, he searched for something to say, but was finding it impossible to transition from funeral to anything else without sounding completely insensitive.

"Kevin wants me to sell the house."

"He what? But he can't. What if it sells quickly? You have school and the clinic and…"

"His brain doesn't work like that. It never has."

"Well, if that's the case, then you can stay with us."

His words were met with silence.

Swallowing, he quickly added, "What I meant to say was, you have options, that is, if you want to stay."

She turned to face him. "Of course I want to stay."

He released his breath. "Have you had a chance to speak to the university about deferring your start?"

"I have an appointment with someone in admissions on

Wednesday. I guess I will have to wait and see what happens."

Reaching across, he gently took her hand in his. "You are going to make it through this, Kate." He felt her fingers tense at his words.

She stared down at their hands. "When you were away, I would sometimes look up at the night sky and search out the brightest star, and wonder if it was possible you might be looking at the same star." She lifted her eyes. "How amazing would that be, sharing the same star at the same moment with someone thousands of miles away?" She held his eyes for a few seconds, then followed them as they narrowed toward some point in the sky. "Shooting star?"

Shaking his head, he held up his thumb as though trying to estimate some distance. Without turning, he said, "Do you see that star, the one that looks a little nearer to us than the rest?"

"Wait a minute, yes, I think I see it. Why? Do you know its name?"

"I'd say it's about three inches to the right of the *Dipper's* tail. Yup, there it is."

"Thank you, Richard, this is all very scientific, especially your measurements."

"You make fun, but I bet you'll never forget that star."

She breathed a quiet sigh. "Probably not."

"I was thinking we might give it a name."

"We can do that?"

"Well, it's hardly official. But as I see it, we all own a piece of the stars, it's our birthright."

"Fair enough, so what would you like to name it?"

"What I was actually thinking was…"

"Go on, what were you thinking?"

"I was thinking how maybe the star could act as a sort of beacon."

"A beacon for what?"

"Maybe beacon was the wrong word." Hesitating, he waited for her to look away, but she didn't oblige him this time; and finding himself unable to manage an eloquent retreat, he swallowed and said, "What I meant was, maybe it can be something you can look toward; something you can always look toward and think of your parents watching over you."

Tilting her head back, she stared up at the star.

Watching, as emotion cast its melancholy shade over the tragic beauty of her moonlit profile, he wanted desperately to take her in his arms, and hold her tight, and take the pain away; but he froze, uncertain of how to physically breach the seemingly impenetrable barrier of grief that stood between them.

She was first to speak. And when she spoke, the fragility he heard in her voice lent to her words the impression of articulated tears.

"Mom used to say, '*A soul gone from earth is a star born in heaven.*'"

"Of that I have no doubt."

Turning, her watery eyes met his eyes with a sad smile.

"I get the feeling your trip changed you somehow."

"I think you may be right."

"Anything you want to share?"

He nodded. "Yes, but not tonight."

CHAPTER NINETEEN

His words were met with silence. And not yet knowing Dr. Alex Toreli well enough to confidently interpret his silences, Richard Sinclair instead, simply lowered his eyes and began reading over his notes.

"Forgive me Richard, I am afraid my thoughts stalled when you were speaking about its resistance to antibiotics."

"Is this something you've seen before?"

"Me personally? No. But I have been reading about an increased incidence of such cases in the literature." Cradling his coffee cup in his hands, Dr. Toreli stared down into it, deliberating. After a few seconds, he lifted his eyes. "The problem with antibiotics is people have become increasingly negligent with how they are being prescribed, taken, manufactured and even disposed of. In fact, it may be suggested that such negligence is contributing to the creation of resistant strains like the one you've just described."

Richard's folded hand slid from his cheek to his chin as he stared thoughtfully into the surface of the workbench. "Oscar didn't mention antibiotics by name, but considering what he said about the supplements they manufacture preventing sickness in cattle, I guess it would make sense." He looked across at Alex. "So I take it you are referring to the grates in the reservoir?"

Alex responded with a nod, but in truth, his mind was elsewhere. Having committed himself to broaching this subject, he was now too involved in the trajectory of his own thoughts to slow their momentum. "But what if there existed a safe and natural alternative?"

"Sorry?"

"An alternative to antibiotics, and one which through its very essence was incapable of posing such a risk."

"I imagine if such a thing existed, we would already be using it."

"It most certainly does exist," said Alex, nodding emphatically. "It exists, and has been used for many years back home."

"Back home?"

"In Tbilisi, in Georgia." Pausing, he held Richard's eyes intently, speculating on how his as yet unspoken words were about to be received. "What would you say if I told you bacterial infections could be treated effectively with viruses?"

"I would say if viruses are involved, the probability of creating resistant bacterial strains is likely to be increased not decreased."

Alex's eyes glinted a smile. "Ah yes, but consider for a moment how it is bacteriophages replicate in nature."

"They infect a bacterial host, but—"

"Exactly, and what happens to the bacterial host in the process?"

"That depends on how the phages replicate. And considering the risks posed when viral DNA integrates into the bacterial genome, not to mention the lengthy dormancy period, I can't see any practical therapeutic application for lysogenic phages."

"And that is precisely why only lytic phages are used. It really is quite beautiful in its simplicity, the way they are able to take over the bacterial host's resources, leaving a trail of ruptured cells in their wake."

"Beautiful, sure, if indeed they pose no harm to us."

"I can assure you they do not."

"Are you saying this is something you've tried? But how were they administered?"

"Yes, and it depends. For common ailments they were purchased, 'over the counter' you might say from a chemist. Alternatively, a swab could be taken in order to develop a therapy targeted against a specific pathogen."

"And this actually works?"

"Well, I am sitting here across from you and am very much

alive." Alex's wide grin slowly straightened into a serious line as he brought his hands together beneath his chin. "It is interesting to note, that prior to the discovery of penicillin, phages were widely used to treat all manner of bacterial infections."

"And yet their therapeutic application was abandoned."

"In the West, yes."

"Why was that?"

"One of the properties which make phages difficult from an industrial perspective is their specificity. With phages, we are not talking in terms of broad-spectrum and narrow-spectrum." Lifting his eyes to the ceiling, he paused for a moment to collect his thoughts. "Consider this, I've heard it said that people who drank the water from the *Ganges* river were resistant to an outbreak of cholera, not because the water was pure, quite the opposite in fact. It was because the contaminated water they were drinking also contained a high concentration of cholera specific phages." Folding his arms across his chest, he arched his brow. "Now tell me Richard, how does one go about patenting such an entity as this?"

Richard stared down at his notes. The writing on the page before him blurred as he considered Alex's words in relation to the pathogen he was investigating.

"Your instincts guided you well," said Alex, glancing up as he read through the list of items on the packing slip.

Richard's body tensed. He had just been thinking along the same lines himself. "What you were just saying about the *Ganges*, about cholera, does that mean it's possible one of those samples might lead not only to the pathogen's source, but also to its cure?"

"In theory, yes, it is possible. But remember, even if found, there exists the very real possibility the corresponding phages for this pathogen may be lysogenic." Alex reached inside his lab coat pocket and turned off the alarm on the timer. "And now, I am afraid I must get back to my lab, but if you would like, I can free up some time tomorrow afternoon to assist with the phages extraction."

"I don't know what to say, Alex. You've given me new hope."

With the corners of his dark pink lips downturned into a faint smile of contentment, Alex quietly said, "I am happy to help."

CHAPTER TWENTY

Perhaps if he had known Thomas Blackwell better, the news of his passing would have been met with a profound sense of sadness. Instead, it was met with a profound sense of unease. Setting the newspaper aside, Phillip Madden's thoughts now concentrated on how this news was going to affect the plans he had set into motion. His stomach tightened and twisted as he envisioned himself having the conversation he had been avoiding for months.

Being a decisive man by nature, he had always loathed introspection. Primarily because he had never seen any advantage gained by allowing time to alter the perception of his actions. How could he possibly fault himself for a decision that had, at the time, been made to ensure Richard's interests were protected? He had acted in earnest; or more accurately, he had convinced himself he was acting in earnest. Is there a difference? Does intent matter when it has little bearing on the end result?

Though met with stubborn resistance, the truth behind his actions gradually penetrated his wall of denial. Staring out at the rising sun, now perched on the horizon, as though awaiting its cue, his rationalizations slowly began to reveal themselves as nothing more than flimsy excuses for his own cowardice. It was a difficult truth to accept. And yet, he could find no valid argument to defend his actions. No matter how hard he tried to spin excuses in his head, in his heart, he knew—he had always known—it was a selfish act to involve Richard in his plans.

Straightening, he gave his head a quick shake and reminded

himself how it served no purpose to dwell on hindsight. There was simply no going back. He had made his decision and now had to face the consequences.

Reaching across his desk for the phone, he dialed through to James Sinclair's office at the hospital.

"Hello," said James, a second time.

"Sorry James, I was expecting your voice mail."

"Is everything okay?"

"James, have you seen today's paper?"

"No, I just got in. Why?"

"Thomas Blackwell has passed away.... I am truly sorry, James."

James was silent.

"Give me a call later if you need to talk, okay?"

The silence on the other end was broken abruptly as the line disconnected.

SLOWLY STRETCHING HIS neck from side to side, Richard Sinclair's eyes moved from Dr. Jon Monteiro's patient files, stacked neatly on the edge of his desk, across to the refrigerator, and then down to his watch. Feeling restless, he stood up, stretched his legs, and began pacing back and forth. Hearing the door open, he froze.

Meeting his anxious eyes with a reassuring smile, Dr. Alex Toreli handed him a cup of coffee. "I know it all seems a little overwhelming right now, but we will figure it out." He then glanced toward Richard's desk. "How did you make out with the kinase application? Were you able to find all the information you needed?"

Nodding, Richard held the cup to his nose and breathed in the aroma. "There were only a few things I couldn't find, but we can discuss them later." He blew on the coffee before taking a large sip. "I should have something ready for you to review by the end of the week."

"That soon?"

"I tend to work quickly when I am using one thing as a means to distract myself from another."

"Well then," said Alex, turning to lock the door, "it is best we get started."

Reaching inside an open box on the workbench, Richard removed two packaged Biohazard suits and handed one to Alex.

"Will you be seeking outside assistance with the pathogen's identification?" said Alex, crouching down to pull the shoe covers over his feet.

"Dr. Monteiro has already had samples sent out to a private lab in the UK."

"I get the sense there's a 'but' in there."

"Maybe," said Richard, his head swaying a slow bob and weave. "Last night, I came across a group here in Montréal using variations in a specific region of DNA to distinguish between species of Mycobacterium. They are using this information to assemble a phylogenetic tree. I had planned on giving them a call this morning, but then my uncle said to leave it with him."

"Does he know someone from the group?"

"The Lead Investigator, a Dr. Halperin."

"Dr. Rachel Halperin?"

"Yes, do you know her too?"

"Only by reputation. She is very well respected in her field, and as I understand, a very attractive woman as well."

"I guess that explains why he was so eager to make the call."

Smiling, Alex gave him a curious look. "You said you came across this group last night? My god, when do you find time to sleep?"

"I'm still a little jet lagged. Though, in truth, my mind was reeling after our conversation yesterday. I really do appreciate you setting aside the time for this."

"It is enough you are helping with the clinical trial application, I detest writing those things. Besides, I am fairly confident Kate has everything under control in the lab."

"Kate? She's here? But her arm?"

"I know, and I tried to persuade her to go home, but she said staying busy helps her to keep her mind off things… and, well, I didn't have the heart to argue with her."

"Of course, I'm sorry. I didn't mean to raise my voice."

"There is no need to apologize," said Alex, his eyes sharpening as he looked down at the collection tubes. Picking one up, he glanced at the label. "Well, the first thing we are going to have to do is isolate the pathogen from these sputum samples."

Shaking his head, Richard groaned a sigh. "I could have sworn I'd asked him to include a sample of the purified pathogen."

"Come now, Richard, don't dismay. As is often the case, necessity has forced us to choose the more logical approach. Waiting until tomorrow will enable us to first check on the samples you have already plated before proceeding; and that, in turn will save us time by narrowing down our search."

"And if all the samples I collected test negative?"

"Then necessity will force us to approach this from a different angle. You must learn to temper your nature with a bit of spontaneity. Successful research is as much about chance as is it about design."

CHAPTER TWENTY-ONE

Reading the error message on the computer screen, Richard Sinclair picked up the phone and dialed his uncle's number.

"Are you sure you entered the password correctly?"

"It's like I said, the message was on the screen when it booted up."

"Do you need to use the computer tonight?"

"No, it can wait. Actually…"

"Actually, what?"

"Sorry, I didn't realize how late it was. Kate's shift is nearly over, and I'm supposed to be picking her up."

"Well then, you had better get going. I will have a look at the computer in the morning."

"I HAVEN'T BEEN by here since they built the new facility. It's actually quite nice."

Staring down into her folded hands, Kate Mironov made no response.

Richard Sinclair glanced at her with a sad smile. "I imagine people are more likely to consider adoption when it doesn't look like a dilapidated prison for wayward animals."

She nodded, but did not speak.

"How was your day?"

"Fine."

"How's your arm?"

"Fine."

"How did your meeting with admissions go?"

"Fine."

A few seconds passed before she lifted her eyes and turned to face him. "Richard, I... I..."

"What is it, Kate? Has something happened?"

She slowly shook her head.

He had experienced her monosyllabic replies before, but this was different. Something in her halting manner, something he had never seen before, was sounding an intuitive alarm. His throat tightened. His mouth went dry. Swallowing, he drew a shaky breath and prepared himself for the worst: *Richard, I'm moving back to San Francisco. Richard, there's this guy at the clinic. Richard, I...* He blinked when heard her voice.

"I need to know how you view our relationship."

"Our relationship? Why? What brought this on all of a sudden?"

She shrugged.

"Did something happen at work today?"

Drawing her brow, she shook her head. "No, no, it's nothing like that. It's just that... you never... you've never..." her voice, already a tremulous whisper, trailed off.

He held his breath: *Never what?*

"I know it makes no sense, you only just got back. And I know how busy you are with work, and how everything's been so heavy and dark. I know that, I do. But then I think how even before the accident, even before everything got so complicated, even then you never." She turned away, and again stared down into her folded hands.

In the silence that followed, Richard's lips parted, but he was at a loss for words. The only two clinging to his tongue were: *Never what?* And his intuition was cautioning him against voicing that thought directly.

Then, without lifting her eyes, and in a voice barely above a whisper, she said, "It's just that sometimes, late at night when I'm all alone and wondering where you are, I think you... about us. And sometimes, my thoughts are so overwhelming, I think surely you must be able to sense them. But you never do. And after hours of thinking and waiting and willing you to knock on the door, or throw a rock against the window—like they do in the movies—I eventually fall asleep. And when I wake the next morning, I have this feeling like I should be angry with you about something, but I'm not sure what."

"Ah... I see," he said, swallowing back the unfamiliar sensation of feeling flattered at the expense of someone else's awkwardness. "Believe me Kate, it's not that I haven't thought about it." He cringed at his words. "It's just that, well, with everything—" He broke off when she lifted her eyes, and with a look, conveyed to him that his words were missing the mark. He gently tucked a strand of hair behind her ear. And looking deep into her eyes, he searched for some indication of what it was she needed to hear him say. "You know," he said softly, his fingers resting gently against the warmth of her skin, "sometimes I lose myself completely when I look into your eyes." He felt a shiver run through her shoulders. And as he stared into her melting eyes, his inhibitions receded. Moving closer, his hesitation was deliberate. His heart was beating madly, intensifying his senses; and yet, it felt as though he was dreaming. Dreaming the sort of dream from which he never wanted to wake. Their lips at first barely touching, he lingered, breathing in her breath.

Then, gently pulling away, he turned and started the car. "There is something I need to show you."

"DID ALEX LEAVE his car here?"

"No, he left before me."

"Do you know who the other car belongs to?"

Craning his neck to see where Kate Mironov was pointing, Richard Sinclair shook his head.

"What on earth could he be doing back here at this hour?"

"I have no idea."

Parking behind Dr. Alex Toreli's car, Richard turned to face her. "Maybe you should wait here."

"You're kidding, right?"

Stepping through the side door ahead of her, Richard immediately felt the hairs stand up on the back of his neck. Glancing back, he held a finger to his lips. They both looked across the foyer and up the stairs. It seemed almost too quiet and too dark. After rummaging around behind the reception desk, he stepped back to her side, armed with a large stapler.

"Really?" she whispered, watching as he clumsily firmed his

grip on the makeshift weapon.

"Do you have a better suggestion?"

Opening her purse, she removed a small canister and handed it to him.

"What's this?"

"Pepper spray. Just hold this button down and aim for the eyes," she said, pointing to the top of the canister.

"You do know this is illegal here, right?"

"And how does Canadian law enforcement feel about bludgeoning someone with a stapler?"

"Okay," he sighed, "but please, just stay close."

They slowly descended the stairs to the basement. Nearing the bottom, they came to an abrupt stop. From beneath the door of his uncle's lab, a horizontal beam of light stretched out across the floor of the hallway.

"Is your uncle here?"

He considered for a moment, then shook his head. Reaching into his pocket, he slipped his car keys into her hand. "If anything happens get to a phone and call the police, okay?"

She nodded.

Edging along the wall, he strained to hear against the sound of his heartbeat thumping in his ears. On the other side of the door a male voice began shouting. Drawing back, he spun around and motioned for Kate to get back up the stairs. Then, gripping his key card in one hand and the canister in the other, he charged through the door.

He froze, gasping as his eyes locked onto Alex, lying on his side with his hands bound behind his back, and an overturned chair on the floor beside him. Alex's eyes flashed with a warning. Readying the canister in his palm, Richard swallowed back a painful gulp of dryness and slowly turned.

Shifting his eyes between them, he could see his own panic reflected in theirs. Suddenly, one of them grabbed a glass beaker from the workbench and hurled it at his head. Ducking out of the way, he spun around just as the glass slammed into the corner of the desk, shattering onto the floor. In the instant it took him to react, they were out the door.

Tearing out behind them, he ran up the stairs and out the side door. As soon as he reached the parking lot he stopped in his tracks; the fear of what might happen were he to catch up to them, suddenly striking his limbs motionless. High beams blared in his eyes as their car sped past, kicking up loose gravel as it skidded through a sharp turn out of the lot.

"*HERE GET THIS* down you," said Kate Mironov, gently placing a glass of water in Dr. Alex Toreli's trembling hands. She frowned at the gash across his cheek. "Is anything broken?"

He shook his head.

Richard was silent as he looked around the lab, unable to move past the sickening feeling his privacy had been violated. With the initial surge of panic now receding, anger was quickly filling its void.

Walking over to the freezer, Kate removed an ice-pack and wrapped it in a hand towel.

"Alex," she said softly, placing the compress into his hands. "Do you think you are well enough to explain what happened?"

"I... I... couldn't sleep. So... so... I came in to get caught up on some work."

"How did you end up in here?" Richard's clenched jaw barely moved as he spoke.

"I was upstairs when they came in," said Alex, lifting the compress to his cheek. "They brought me down here. They had a key card. They did. You must believe me." He looked between them through pleading eyes.

"Of course we believe you," said Kate, casting Richard a critical glance.

No sooner had Richard met her eyes, than he recalled that the key card he had been using since Monday was his uncle's spare copy, his own having been misplaced. He took a step back, unable to think clearly as feelings of guilt vied with lingering suspicions. Breathing a shaky breath, he crossed his arms and looked directly at Alex. "Do you know if there was something specific they were looking for in here?"

Alex slowly shook his head. "They just kept repeating the same question over and over."

"What question?"

"Where is Edward Blackwell?"

"Edward Blackwell?"

"Who is Edward Blackwell?" asked Kate.

"He's my uncle's business partner."

"They said he was here, I mean in Montréal. I told them I knew nothing. I told them he has not stepped foot in this building for as long as I have worked here. But they kept insisting I knew where to find him."

"Do you know if Edward is in town?"

Alex's features pulled tight, as though offended by the question. "I have no idea," he said, quickly lowering his eyes.

Turning, Richard swept his eyes across the room. Pausing at the shards of shattered glass on the floor, he said, "Do you remember if they were wearing gloves?"

"I think so, but I also clearly remember his ring slicing across my cheek."

Richard breathed a quiet sigh. "We are going to have to call the police. We will need to file a report and have the lab checked for prints."

Alex's head shot up. Searching Richard's face, he wondered what, if anything, Phillip had told him about his history. "I can't be involved in this."

"What do you mean?"

"I mean with the police. I can't give a statement. I can't testify in court. I can't be involved in any way."

Holding his eyes, now deadly serious, Richard recalled the words, his uncle had spoken about Edward having something over him. And as he stared across at the proud and erudite man, now beaten and humbled and asking for mercy, his every negative emotion was displaced by a sense of pity. "You should probably go home, Alex."

"But what are you going to tell the police?"

"Only what is necessary. Go home Alex. You've been through enough tonight."

CHAPTER TWENTY-TWO

Phillip Madden reached across his desk for the teapot. "The good news is, whoever tried to log onto the computer was unsuccessful."

"And the bad news?"

"We are going to need to push forward with publication. I am afraid it has become a matter of some urgency."

"Urgency?"

Crossing his arms, Phillip's lips tightened into a line as he slowly rocked his head. "I have taken every legal precaution necessary to ensure this work is protected from any claim Edward might try to make. Still, in light of what happened last night, I will not breathe easy until we publish."

"You're not seriously thinking Edward Blackwell sent those two to try to steal your research? But that makes no sense. Why would he involve Alex in such a way? And if Alex is, as you say, in Edward's pocket, why would he say they were looking for him?"

"Because that is exactly the sort of twisted game Edward plays. And if he has been given reason to believe I am keeping something significant from him, then he will stop at nothing to find out what it is."

"So you're thinking it was Alex who tried to log on to the computer?"

"I am certain."

"And my missing key card?"

"If it has managed to find its way into the wrong hands, it will be useless to them after today."

"Were the police able to trace the license plate?"

"The car had been reported stolen."

Lowering his eyes, Richard swallowed. "There's something else I've been wanting to discuss with you."

"Ah yes, the real reason you were here last night."

Straightening his back, Richard's features tightened as guilt competed with denial for control of his expression.

"It's okay Richard. To be honest, I'm surprised you have managed to keep it from her as long as you have."

"I haven't told her anything."

"And now," pausing, Phillip joined his hands beneath his chin and narrowed his eyes. "Oh, I see, so you would like her to assist you."

Richard gave a noncommittal nod and shrug.

"Perhaps you can find a way, without involving her in the particulars of the work, if you know what I mean."

Richard's expression softened. Though there were times when he hated his inability to keep his thoughts from his uncle, there were an equal number of times when it had its advantages. And such are our tendencies that even in that moment, under his uncle's watchful eye, he attempted to hide that very thought behind a sedate smile.

"You know Richard, she truly is a remarkable girl. If I were you I would be—"

"I should be getting back to the lab," said Richard, jumping to his feet.

"Yes, yes, of course." Phillip nodded to himself. "I did tell you I will be flying back out to Maputo on Sunday and will need you to—"

"You what?"

"Sorry Richard, my head's been all over the place."

"But why? We only just got back. Unless…" Richard's expression melted as he sought his uncle's eyes.

"No. Jon wouldn't keep something like that from us."

"Then what is it?"

"It's difficult to explain." Through a quiet sigh, Phillip paused and lowered his eyes. "Yesterday, when I called Jon to tell him about the soil samples testing positive, his reaction was strangely subdued. I could sense he was deliberately holding something back. And when you have known someone for as long as I've known Jon, and have been through what we've been through, well, I just feel I need to be there for him." Lifting his eyes, he met Richard's directly. "You do understand, right?"

"But you did explain about the phages, and that we should have the first set of results tomorrow?"

"Yes, we discussed it at length."

"And was that the 'deliberately holding something back' part of the conversation or did that come later?"

"Don't do this to yourself, Richard. You must try not to take the weight of the world on your shoulders, it leads to nothing but an aching back. Come what may with the phages, you have already accomplished what you set out to do, the rest is out of your hands. Besides, I could be reading this all wrong. I will have a better sense of what is going on when I am able to speak with him face to face."

"So what do you need from me?"

"Sorry?"

"You had started to say you will need something."

"Jon has a meeting scheduled with the Health Ministry next week and since I will now be there—"

"You would like a summary of my findings."

"A photocopy of your notes will suffice. I can compose a summary on the flight over."

GLARING DOWN AT the plate in front of him, Richard Sinclair regarded the lawn of cells with an adversarial sense of loathing. That he had formed a particular attachment to this project was certain. But there was more to it than just his personal sense of responsibility to see it through to the end. It was as though by its very nature, this opponent had awoken some primal drive inside him. The cells he was looking at were alive and lethal, and representative of something against which we could one day find our species fighting for its very survival.

Tilting his head back, he closed his eyes. The stream of his thoughts, both preceding and present, brought a faint smile of embarrassment to his face. It was the sort of internal monologue he would never dare speak aloud. It was the sort of internal monologue that, on this occasion, ended when the words, *Je pense, donc je suis* managed to thread their way to the front of his congested mental landscape. However conjured, the words had their intended effect. If humankind can reason its very existence into being, then surely we can gain the advantage over a tiny microbe. When he looked back down at the plate, he did so through determined eyes.

The feeling of empowerment was fleeting, however. For no sooner had his confidence been bolstered, than did that very human attribute of reason bring him crashing back down to earth. The voice of reason dictating that it would be foolish to believe he could ever truly gain the upper hand over such a microbe, over any microbe for that matter. This was, after all, an arms race; and it was they who had the evolutionary advantage. Giving his head a quick shake, he reached for another pipette and continued adding aliquots of phages to the plates.

Having worked steadily through the afternoon, he was forced to take a break when the increasingly vocal rumblings in his stomach could no longer be ignored. He saw Kate standing against the wall opposite the door when he opened it. She was balancing two large white binders on her cast, holding a paper bag and coffee cup in her other hand, and gripping a second cup by her teeth.

He reached across to free the cup from her teeth and lift the binders from her arm. "Why didn't you knock?"

"Um, because that's a pretty strong deterrent," she said, tilting her head toward the Biohazard sign on the door. "Is it safe for me to come in?"

"Yup, we're all clear."

Taking a tentative step inside, her eyes swept cautiously across the room.

"That cast should be coming off soon shouldn't it?"

"Not soon enough."

"What's in the binders?"

"New security protocols," she said, frowning at the dark circles beneath his eyes.

"I'm fine. I just need to drink enough coffee so it becomes physiologically impossible for me to close my eyes."

"That's a comforting thought." Reaching into her pocket, she handed him a new key card. "Geneviève asked me to give this to you."

"Thanks. Oh and Kate, before I forget, I wanted to ask you about Henry. He left a strange message on my voice mail."

"I didn't mean to say anything."

"Huh?"

"It's just that, well, for some reason he was asking me if you had found your key card. And then, that conversation led to me telling him about last night. And then, well, he didn't come right out and say it, but the way he was acting I got the impression he thinks he might know something about what happened."

Richard was silent.

Lowering her eyes, she took a step back. "I'm sorry Richard, it all just kind of slipped out."

"It's okay, Kate. You haven't done anything wrong. Henry has enough sense not to go around accusing people of things. If he knows something, he will play it smart."

Tightening her lips, she gave him a slight nod and held out the bag in her hand. "Have you had any lunch?"

"I was just on my way down to grab something," he said, reaching an eager hand inside the bag. "But this is great, thanks."

"No problem. Well, I better get back."

"Oh, and Kate."

Turning, she arched her brow.

"It's nothing urgent, but I could really use your help tonight if you have time."

"I have time. What do you need help with?"

"It's a bit of a long story."

"Does this have anything to do with what you wanted to show me yesterday?"

He nodded.

"Okay, how about we meet at the pub next door around six and you can explain everything?"

"Sounds good."

Stopping at the door, she looked back over her shoulder. "I am really sorry about Henry. I honestly didn't mean to stir up trouble."

"I know. And there is no need to apologize."

STANDING IN THE corner at the back of room 306, Henry

Sinclair could feel his blood simmering beneath his skin. Crossing his arms, he positioned his tense body flush against the cold concrete wall. All he could think about was what a fool he had been to allow them into his home.

He waited for the others to leave before peeling himself off the wall and approaching the front of the room. With Adèle Leary standing attentively at his side, Jack Doherty glanced up from the papers in his hand and met his eyes directly. Had he not by now grown accustomed to Jack's deliberately severe, almost challenging expression, it would have easily been enough to set him off.

"You didn't mention anything during the meeting, so I figured you hadn't yet heard."

"Heard what?"

"Blackwell Laboratories was broken into last night."

"Well, I guess there's always a risk of that happening," said Adèle, her tone flat with forced disinterest.

Henry caught Jack flash her a warning glance. "They roughed up one of the employees pretty badly."

"Is that right?" Jack's tone was casual. "Probably just some junkies. They must have thought the building was empty."

"Yeah," said Adèle. "He must have startled them and they panicked."

Pulling his brow, Henry tilted his head and gave her a questioning look. "Did I say the employee was a guy?"

The little color there was in her naturally pallid complexion suddenly drained from her cheeks.

"Settle down *Columbo*, it's a figure of speech," said Jack, avoiding the apology in Adèle's eyes as he turned toward the door.

"Shame though," said Henry, now speaking to their backs. "He's pretty shaken up. They don't know if he'll be able to return to work."

Stopping in the doorway, Jack looked back over his shoulder. "Was there something else?"

Holding his eyes, Henry slowly shook his head.

HAVING RETURNED FROM the pub, Kate Mironov was now seated at Richard Sinclair's desk reading through the dog eared pages of the *Asclepius* folder. In an almost reverential silence, her fingers carefully turned each page over as though they comprised some ancient manuscript. Lifting her eyes, she met Richard's with an expression that left no doubt she had grasped the magnitude of his uncle's discovery. Stretching her arm across the desk, she turned on the monitor and opened a new spreadsheet.

Seated at the workbench across from her, Richard stared vacantly into the screen of his laptop. Procrastination soon bred the impulse to glance over at her every few seconds. His inability to concentrate on his own work now felt magnified by the ease with which she had delved into hers. He wondered how simultaneously experiencing feelings of resentment and admiration would read on his expression were she to look up and catch him staring.

After several false starts, his fingers finally aligned with his brain and found their way to the keyboard. Before long, he had fallen into such a steady pace that two hours passed by as though an instant.

Lifting his dry eyes from the screen, he arched his stiff back and stretched his arms over his head, releasing several pained groans in the process.

Turning in her chair, she grinned at him. "Are you going to make it?"

"Sorry about that," he said, brushing a hand across his sheepish smile. "We'd better get going if we're going to catch the last train."

CHAPTER TWENTY-THREE

Phillip Madden stared at his computer screen through distracted eyes. His mind was preoccupied. He had begun the introduction of the paper easily enough. In fact, he had been quite pleased with his steady progress. But then the phone had rung. And glancing at the number, he knew he had to take the call.

And now, with his attention divided, the letters on the screen appeared as unrecognizable symbols. Characters swaying and shifting and warping, as lines of text blurred and blended with numbers and chemical formulas. Closing his eyes, he lifted his fingers to his temples and with their warm tips, pressed gentle circles to soothe the aching pulse.

Vaguely recalling a phrase he had jotted down weeks prior, he began scouring through his notes. He clearly remembered having written the words down, and yet, it was as though they had vanished. He ran his fingers over each line, searching for this lost phrase; its very elusiveness increasing its relevance with each turned page. A heavy knock on his office door interrupted his train of thought.

For some time the two men took measure of each other, guarded eyes piercing through the heavy silence that filled the room.

The passage of time had done nothing to abate the animosity Phillip felt for the shadowy figure now standing before him. His stillness seemed impossible, as though he were some imagined phantom, summoned from hell to torment him. A flood of painful memories, long ago relegated to the past, now rushed to the surface, sending a bone chilling shiver coursing through his body. He could taste the bile rising in his throat, but sat motionless, dumbstruck and defenseless against the sudden onslaught of emotions.

He found the peculiarity of Edward Blackwell's appearance almost as unnerving as his unwelcome presence. It was as though the corruption within had been laid bare, manifest upon his face. The patrician attractiveness was still vaguely present; but now, a receding hairline accentuated the high forehead. And the face itself appeared almost too angular, as though the skin was pulled impossibly tight around his skull. Phillip felt revulsion; and yet, he could not bring himself to look away, regarding him now through a lens of colliding impressions: everything that was and everything he would never allow to be again.

"I am disappointed in you Phillip. I would have thought my presence not entirely unexpected."

Phillip cringed as his ears registered the honeyed intonation of Edward's voice. Bracing his hands against his desk, tension spread through to the tips of his fingers, his nails piercing the wood finish. He felt the heightened sense of visceral awareness present in the seconds before rage manifests. Anything blocking the path between Edward and himself faded to background as his vision tunneled. And in an instant, instinct defied intellect.

Adrenaline coursing through his veins, he sprang up from his chair and lunged at Edward, hoisting him against the wall. Then, with a force borne of two decades of pent up resentment, he hurled his clenched fist into Edward's leathery jaw.

Folded over, Edward slowly tilted his head to face him. Phillip stared him down through raging eyes. Every primal instinct was urging him on. He needed to have this out. But Edward held out his hand, and with an unyielding look, made clear his refusal to fight.

"Ah yes, I remember now," said Phillip, snorting as he turned. "You never were up for a fair fight, were you?" Walking on unsteady legs, he mustered his last ounce of strength to avoid collapsing into his chair. He felt weak all over. His body trembled as the initial surge of adrenaline dropped, leaving him with an acute awareness of the pain: cold and dense and throbbing in his knuckles.

"Do you feel any better now?" Edward's words garbled as he stretched out his jaw.

"Not even close."

Brushing himself off, Edward walked to the chair opposite Phillip's desk. Pausing, he pulled it out a few feet before seating himself. A drop of blood trickled down his chin. "It has been a long time," he said, dabbing it away with his handkerchief.

"As I recall," said Phillip, intent upon inflicting more pain. "It was the day I was supposed to meet Abby for dinner to celebrate the news of her pregnancy."

The skin around Edward's eyes twitched as he fought to maintain a composed façade.

"Ah, I see," continued Phillip, leaning forward, eyes narrowing. "You did not know she was pregnant."

Rising to his feet, Edward walked across the room. With his back to Phillip, he stood in front of the bookshelf. "Is it possible you have finally managed to find your backbone, Phillip?"

"She had a miscarriage." Phillip's words, as though delivered upon the edge of a hatchet blade, cut their serrated path through the air. "Though I've learned that sometimes happens when someone endures a severe trauma in the early stages of pregnancy."

Steadying himself, Edward's trembling hands gripped the edge of the bookshelf.

"What? Have you nothing to say? Come now, Edward, it's not like you to give up so easily."

Edward resisted, biting down hard on his tongue to ensure he would not betray himself. And as he swallowed back the salty rush of blood, seeping from the self-inflicted wound, he held firm, refusing to submit. He was silent for several seconds before slowly turning. He gave his watch a casual glance. "It is nearly time for lunch, let us not poison our palates with foul words."

"If you wanted to avoid having this conversation, then you should have never come back. That was the deal, was it not?"

"I'm afraid things have changed."

"I assume you are referring to your father's passing."

"Yes, well, even the great Thomas Blackwell cannot evade the inevitability of death."

"Huh."

"Huh, what?"

"With your father's passing, I would have thought you'd have neither the time nor the… Unless…" Folding his arms across his chest, Phillip narrowed his eyes. "No," he sighed. "You would never sell me your shares. You enjoy tormenting me far too much to relinquish your hold."

Making no reply, Edward helped himself to the bottle of scotch on the bookshelf and returned to the chair. Cradling the crystal glass in his palm, he eyed Phillip carefully, wondering to what degree, if any, he may have underestimated him. "And how is Richard working out?"

Phillip's fist came down hard on his desk, causing his teacup to clatter against its saucer. "I don't have time for this nonsense," he growled. "What is it you want?"

Edward's pointed lips curled into a gloating smirk. "Settle down Phillip, I was merely offering you the opportunity to explain."

"Explain what?"

"To explain why he is using company resources to investigate an isolated outbreak in some remote—" He broke off as his glance fell upon the airline ticket on the corner of Phillip's desk. "And now I see you will be travelling again. Do you really think that is wise?"

Phillip did not respond. He could see the wheels turning, but held his tongue, his thoughts now concentrated on how he was going to keep Richard protected in his absence. And as he searched for and abandoned several implausible countermeasures, quite unexpectedly, it was Edward who provided the solution.

"Since I now have a vested interest in how this project develops, I think it would be best if I accompany you on this trip."

Resisting the reflex to open his mouth in protest, Phillip sank back in his chair, acknowledging that despite his own misgivings, it would be safer to have Edward where he could keep an eye on him.

"Besides, as it happens, I have other business in Marsiquet which could benefit from some face time."

"It always seemed to me a rather strange choice of location to build a chemical plant."

"How strange things appear often depends on one's perspective." Edward smirked through his words. "Come now Phillip, don't look so dismayed. You may actually find my particular talents even more beneficial than those of your brilliant young nephew."

"Edward, it is important this project is kept above board. I don't want any backroom dealings tainting it."

"I promise I will not do anything to compromise the integrity of your little project. All the same, you are more naive than I thought if..." Heeding Phillip's warning stare, he did not finish his thought aloud.

BETWEEN HER FINGERS, Kate Mironov swayed a steam-stained paper bag from the boulangerie across the street. "Are you hungry?"

Richard Sinclair grinned his eager reply, grateful the savory aroma had not been a conjuring of his rumbling stomach.

"And I'm guessing I don't need to ask if you want this," she added, setting the coffee cup down on the workbench beside him.

"Thanks Kate. I didn't know you were coming in today. Is Alex here?"

"No, Geneviève said he will be back on Monday." She stepped toward the window and glanced outside. Then, turning, she swept her eyes across the lab. Meeting his, she grinned and walked back toward him. Lifting her finger, she wiped a drop of cream cheese from the corner of his mouth. She then held his eyes; her own, now flickering with curiosity.

He responded with an arched brow, his tongue being otherwise engaged in dislodging a poppy seed from between his front teeth.

"Have you checked on them yet?"

"No, not yet, but I was just about to." Washing down the last bite with a mouthful of coffee, he reached into the cupboard above his head and handed her a packaged Biohazard suit. "Here, you're going to need to put this on if you're sticking around."

Her eyes lit up. "You don't mind?"

"Of course not," he said, moving past her to lock the door.

WITH HIS ELBOWS propped on the outer edge of the stainless steel Biosafety cabinet, Richard Sinclair breathed a quiet sigh, picked up the plate, he had just set down, and tilted it toward Kate. "Can you see okay?" Without waiting for her reply, he angled the plate away from the light reflecting off the glass shield. "They are plaques, areas where the phages have lysed the bacterial cells."

"Does that mean what I think it means?"

"It means we have found our phages, yes, but there's an inconsistency that's bothering me." Breathing another quiet sigh, he stared down at the plate.

Seeing the inward look in his eyes, Kate waited for him to come back. But when several seconds passed and he still had yet to speak, she cleared her throat and said, "Inconsistency?"

He blinked; and then, like a record whose needle had just been adjusted, he continued with the same tone and pace as before his pause. "The phages applied to each quadrant of this plate were derived from four soil samples collected a few feet apart. And yet, only one soil sample contained the corresponding phages." Setting the plate back down, he slowly moved his eyes over the others, aligned across the surface of the cabinet. "What's more, out of the twenty soil samples I collected, only three contained the corresponding phages."

"And when you tested the soil samples for the pathogen?"

"These same three were positive."

"I see," she said, in a tone suggesting the opposite. "And how is that inconsistent?"

"In and of itself, it's not. But you know how sometimes you have to view something from a different angle in order to see it as it truly is?"

"Sure."

"It's not the low statistic per se, but rather its significance. What I mean is, it's inconsistent with my working theory for how the microbe came to be present in the soil."

"Which was what?"

"It centered on the water used to irrigate the soil becoming contaminated by waste from a nearby chemical plant. And how, over time, the contaminated water had altered the chemistry of bacteria present in the soil. But if a situation like that had occurred, I would have expected the altered microbes to be distributed differently to what we're seeing." Pausing, he turned and held her eyes. "I had become so convinced the chemical plant was somehow involved, that I came up with a theory to support my conclusion; and in the process, I managed to overlook the obvious."

"Sorry Richard, but nothing about this seems obvious to me."

"We're dealing with a strain of *M. bovis*."

"Okay, and…?"

"What if the bacteria was shed in the feces of infected animals, feces that was then used as fertilizer?"

"But I thought you said their livestock had tested negative."

"What if the feces didn't come from their livestock?"

"Wouldn't that have come up when you were talking with them?"

"I never thought to ask."

"And you're saying these results make sense if the pathogen came from fertilizer?"

"More sense than what I was proposing with the water; especially, if the manure had been collected from both healthy and infected livestock."

"If you're right, would this shed any light on how the victims who didn't come into contact with the soil became infected?"

"In that regard, my working theory still applies. If we assume it was originally contracted by those who tended the crops through breaks in their skin or when they touched their faces. It may have then been passed on to others in a similar manner through contact with residual bacteria on the clothing or person of those returning from the fields."

"Maybe… but if that was the case, doesn't it seem likely the people who took care of them when they became ill would have also been infected?"

"Not necessarily, think about what you come into contact with at the clinic. And then think about what you do as soon as you get home. If you had something on your clothes or skin, it's more likely to transmit to someone brushing up against you at work or on the Métro, than to your family. Especially if its viability is strictly limited."

"Perhaps… I don't know. It all just seems so random. I mean when you think about tuberculosis, you think highly contagious, right?"

"I don't know what to say, Kate. Maybe the mutations that accelerated its lethality, in some way altered its transmissibility. I've read about these sorts of microbes, mere footnotes in pathological history because they strike quickly and then vanish, never to be seen again."

"Mere footnotes yes, provided they don't adapt the ability to be passed through the air."

"If I'm right about this, which my gut is telling me I am, we need to find out where that manure was coming from."

"OH, I'M SORRY, I'll come back later."

"It's okay Richard, he was just leaving."

Quickly rising to his feet, Edward Blackwell approached with his hand extended. "So this is the Richard Sinclair, whom I've heard so much about." He pressed his lips into an appraising smile. "Since your uncle is not going to introduce us, please allow me, I'm Edward Blackwell, and you of course are Richard Sinclair."

"Introduce you? But I believe you have already met. Mind you, he was just a toddler at the time and probably doesn't remember. Then again, perhaps that is for the best."

Richard stood motionless, volleying his glance between them as he shook Edward's still outstretched hand.

"You look as though you have some good news to share," said Edward, returning to the bottle of scotch and refilling his glass. "It's okay Richard, there should be no secrets between us."

Richard shot his uncle questioning look.

Sitting with a stony expression and his arms folded tightly across his chest, Phillip Madden lifted his eyes to the ceiling and inclined his head, just slightly.

"Go on," said Edward, holding the glass up in front of his eyes and inspecting its contents closely.

"We've had some success in treating the plated pathogen with phages isolated from soil samples."

"My compliments, Richard, I have been in your presence for a matter of minutes and already you have lived up to your reputation."

Richard managed a polite smile. "I have to get back to the lab. It was nice to meet you Mr. Blackwell." He did not wait for either man to reply before turning on his heels and hurrying out the door.

CHAPTER TWENTY-FOUR

Easily recognizable with his peculiar aristocratic air, Edward Blackwell stood out amongst the crowd of monochromatic suits as he exited *Place Ville Marie.*

Drawing a sharp breath, Jack Doherty jumped to his feet. But no sooner was he vertical than he froze, the months of planning and anticipation now hindering his ability to act.

Following his eyes, Adèle knew in an instant the moment they had been waiting for had finally arrived. There was simply no mistaking him. Placing her hand on Jack's shoulder, she gave him a slight nod.

Dodging the traffic, they trailed Edward as he crossed René Lévesque and headed toward the entrance of the *Fairmont.* Once through the doors, he started in the direction of the elevators. Stopping midway, he turned and approached the front desk.

They now stood a few feet behind him, straining against the din of pedestrian traffic to hear a mention of his room number. Edward's one-sided conversation with the apologetic hotel manager ended abruptly when he turned his back and resumed his path toward the elevators. Keeping her head down, Adèle followed. She stopped at the entrance to the dimly lit alcove and reached for a brochure from the display rack. When the elevator doors closed behind him, she lifted her eyes over the glossy page and watched as the numbers lit up his ascent.

"Did you get his room number?"

"Sorry Jack, I panicked at the thought of being alone with him in that elevator. But it stopped on the fourteenth floor."

Jack nodded. "Did you happen to catch any of his conversation with the hotel manager?"

"You mean about his 'client' having been detained by hotel security."

"I guess the old boy still has some life left in him."

"Were you able to learn anything from the manager?"

"Nope, but I did make a reservation."

She was about to ask him if the reservation was really necessary, when he gave her a look which made her think better of questioning him.

The expression Jack saw on her face caused him concern. He had seen the look before: middle class girls from respectable families looking for something to rebel against, who then get cold feet the second things exceed their comfort zone. But he had truly thought Adèle was different.

"Whose name did you use to book the room?" The question escaped her lips before she could moderate her anxious tone.

"What do you take me for?"

She shook her head: a short and rapid flutter.

"I booked the room for my dear old grandfather, who will be visiting from Ireland."

"But don't you need a credit card to make a reservation?"

He shot her another cautioning look. "Listen Adèle, you had better let me know right now if you're not comfortable with this because once my plans are set in motion, I will have no time to deal with someone questioning my every move."

"Please try to remember this is all new to me, Jack." Her voice was thin and quivering.

He nodded, but withheld the look of understanding she was searching for in his eyes. Then, turning, he walked back toward the hotel entrance.

She followed behind him. When they reached the door, she placed her hand on his arm and waited for him to turn before speaking. "And what are we going to do about Henry?"

"Well, I guess we'll just have to make it impossible for him to interfere."

She lowered her eyes.

Her question reminding him of the risks involved should her

loyalty wane, he softened his tone. "What is it Adèle?"

"Perhaps if he knew the truth."

"And if you're wrong?"

"*IT WAS DURING* our post-graduate studies that Edward Blackwell approached your father and me with the idea of starting up this company. I imagine it seemed a convenient way for him to appear industrious in his own right. The plan was, he would provide the backing and the contacts, and James and I would conduct the research."

"Dad?"

Arching his brow, Phillip Madden drew in his chin. "Without your father and his development of *Xenestron*, this company would have never matured beyond its inception."

"But this makes no sense. I went to him for advice before accepting your offer and he said nothing about having worked here. He had to have known I'd find out. Why would he have kept this from me?"

"When I approached your parents with my intentions, well, you must understand they had put this all behind them and there I was reopening old wounds. But I promised them you would be protected."

"Put what all behind them? Protected from what?"

"Working alongside someone like you, and like your father before you, people with a seemingly effortless ability, it can place a rather unpleasant magnifying glass on one's own inadequacies. And at the time, misguided as I was, I actually shared a sense of empathy with Edward."

"With Edward? What? Please, just tell me what happened."

Phillip hesitated. His throat felt like sandpaper, its grit conspiring with his unwillingness to say the words he needed to say. "Edward had James's name removed from the research submitted for publication and from everything connected to the development of *Xenestron*."

"But how is that even possible?"

"He reduced your father's involvement to that of a minor contributor."

"And you did nothing to intervene on dad's behalf?"

"Through my failure to act I was complicit."

"Surely you must have recognized it was unethical."

Phillip felt sick inside. The sleepless nights had in no way prepared him to be on the receiving end of the disappointment he now saw in his nephew's eyes. "To this day, I still don't understand how he managed to convince me his actions were justified."

"Perhaps you wanted to believe him."

The icy words sent a shiver over Phillip's skin. Swallowing back the lump in his throat, he said, "I was naive and impressionable and Edward seized upon my weaknesses. At the time, I think I would have believed anything he had said."

"And mom, was she with dad when all this was going on?"

Nodding, Phillip stared into his hands. "I've never seen anything like the infatuation Edward had for Abby. It was like he wanted to possess her. And when she tried to explain that she did not share his feelings—that she was in love with James—he considered her rejection an act of betrayal. And with his demented mind hard set on revenge, he chose to hurt her the only way he could, by hurting James." Pausing, he ran an ice cold palm across his forehead. "I now look back on that time in my life and find myself completely unrecognizable. But that is what Edward does, he breaks people's spirits for the sport of it. The subtlety of his manipulation does not lessen its intended effect, and when he's finished, you're lucky if you can escape with some semblance of your former self intact."

"I'm almost afraid to ask what it was that finally changed your mind about him."

Phillip hesitated. Though he hated having to lie—especially in the middle of a confession—he knew he had no choice. "There just came a point when I could no longer deny the truth of who he was."

"And Edward?"

"Until this morning, I had not laid eyes on him since the day he left town, over twenty years ago."

TILTING HIS HEAD, Jack Doherty softened his features and gave Adèle the look of understanding he knew she was seeking. "Listen Adèle, I know how you feel about Henry, but there's no way he would ever agree to go along with us on this."

She nodded; though in her eyes, he still saw traces of doubt.

"Adèle, we might not get another opportunity like this. It wouldn't be fair of us to put Henry in that kind of position. You do understand that right?"

Again she nodded.

He searched her face as she considered his words and was relieved to see the shadows of doubt receding from her eyes. "I will call the others and tell them we need to meet tonight."

"Everyone?"

"Only those I am certain we can trust."

"How are you going to explain about Henry?"

"Don't worry about that. In fact, it's something I can use to my advantage."

"How so?"

"It's human nature, luv. His exclusion will elevate the importance of their own involvement. It's all in how you spin it."

Cupping his hand around her neck, he pulled her towards him. "I'm sorry to put all this on you luv, but you are the only one I can trust."

"I promise I won't let you down."

Their eyes locked as their lips parted.

"You know what I need you to do now?"

Holding his eyes, she slowly nodded.

CONCEALING HIS TREPIDATION behind lowered eyes, Phillip Madden breathed a quiet sigh and parted his lips to speak. "Before you started here, I had my lawyer draw up something to ensure what happened to your father would never happen to you." Slowly, he lifted his eyes. Meeting Richard's, he saw the disappointment had already receded; though what had taken its place he could not read with certainty. He had not known his nephew's expressive features capable of such inscrutability. And unable to gauge Richard's mindset, he suddenly felt adrift in unchartered waters. Swallowing, he cleared his throat. "Over the years, Edward has grown complacent with my handling of the day to day operations of the business. To the point where, now, company letterhead and an exhaustive budgetary preamble are sufficient to obtain a prompt signature on most documents I send his way. Mind you, in this particular instance, great care had to be taken in the precise phrasing so as not to sound any alarms." Bringing a hand to his brow, Phillip slowly shook his head. "You cannot imagine the sense of relief I felt when Geneviève placed those signed documents on my desk."

"What exactly was it, he signed?"

"A lease agreement for the laboratory space downstairs."

"You mean your lab?"

Phillip nodded. "The Company leasing the space has been operating as a completely separate entity for almost a year now and Blackwell Laboratories has no legal rights to anything they have developed."

Tightening his lips, Richard slowly shook his head. "Payroll," he said, the words spoken low and through the snort of acknowledgement that often accompanies the brain's fitting together of scattered pieces.

"Payroll?"

"On my first day here, you had told me you needed those forms signed for payroll. I remember reading something on one of the pages. I had meant to ask you about it, but kept forgetting. And now, it all makes sense. Or rather, now it raises the questions of: Who do I work for? Who has been depositing money into my bank account? And who has been making the lease payments?"

"Don't worry. It's all above board. On paper you were hired as a consultant."

"And the lease payments?"

"You have been making those. Automatic withdrawal from your business account." Arching his brow, he gave him a wry smile. "Perhaps now, you can understand the reasoning behind what must have seemed an unreasonably inadequate salary."

Bringing his folded hands to his chin, Richard kept the thoughts behind his faint smile to himself. "I can appreciate why you would go to such lengths to protect *Asclepius*, but why wait eight months to tell me about this? It wouldn't have changed anything for me, you must know that."

"Because when you started here, it was little more than an idea in its infancy. An idea that could have just as easily failed as succeeded. And you had so much on your plate already, I didn't want to involve you in the particulars while they were still being worked out. And then, as the weeks turned to months, it just seemed the timing was never right."

"How does your decision to tell me about this now connect with Edward showing up here today?"

"There's more."

"I'm listening."

"I have lined up several investors, like-minded and ethical investors, people whom I have known for years and can trust. They have access to funds which will see *Asclepius* through the preclinical and beyond. But in the short term, until I tie up some loose ends, I must ensure there is no direct connection between myself and the research. And by that I mean, the documentation supplied to the investors was all in your name and has been dated accordingly."

"Dated accordingly? How is that even possible? No one in their right mind is going to believe I've managed that volume of research in just eight months."

"Nor would I expect them to. The original specimens? A curiosity, brought back years ago from my travels and placed in your hands. And yes, you did conduct the majority of your research in the small lab I keep in my home. And yes, I did order you some supplies. And yes, we did discuss your progress. But that was the extent of my involvement, a peripheral advisor. With regard to the *Asclepius* work you have completed over the past eight months, it is documented as is, the dates unaltered. As it happens, the pace with which you have actually progressed, lends credibility to the dates I have amended. Besides, think about it Richard, there's always the possibility that luck intervened; for in truth, years might have been shaved off my efforts had it done so."

"The other work I've done. The other work I'm doing. What is to become of it?"

"As I said, you were hired as a consultant. I have ensured there are no proprietary issues preventing you from continuing with the phages work, *Asclepius* will come with us and everything else stays behind."

"Come with us where?"

"I have someone interested in purchasing my shares in this company. And I anticipate the deal going through by the end of next week."

"Next week?" What happens then?"

"I've put a down-payment on some lab space in the east-end. It is small mind you, but adequate for our purposes."

"When the *Asclepius* paper is published, he's going to put two and two together. Don't you think his lawyers will find a way to get around this?"

"They can try, but they will not succeed. I've made sure of that. Besides, once he realizes his hands are tied, he will no doubt attempt to downplay the situation. Pride will prevent his allowing anyone to think I've gotten the better of him."

Taking his head in his hands, Richard closed his eyes.

"I know I've made a lot of assumptions on your behalf, and if you have any reservations, there is still time to stop what I've set in motion. All I ask is that you—" Breaking off, Phillip turned toward the phone, its ringing interrupting the sequence of both thoughts and words.

NOW SEATED IN one of the two wingback chairs, positioned at angles opposite the elevators, Adèle Leary could see clearly down both corridors on the fourteenth floor.

She kept her eyes fixed on the brochure in her hands, casting casual glances over its pages as a steady stream of business types approached. Reading the smirks on their faces, she could almost hear their thoughts as they looked her up and down.

The seconds passed like minutes. The minutes like hours. Each time the elevator doors opened, her stomach tightened in nervous anticipation of someone questioning her lingering presence. Checking her watch for the umpteenth time, she was filled with dread at the thought of Jack's cold reception should she return to the apartment empty handed.

Just as her anxious eyes lifted from her watch, a door opened and out stepped Edward Blackwell. In his hands he was holding a tea service tray as though he had expected someone to be there, waiting to receive it. She froze like a frightened rabbit when he cast a curious glance down the corridor. She shuddered as her eyes brushed past his, cold and empty. Staring down at the brochure in her trembling hands, her heart seized, terrified that for some reason or other he might approach. Hearing his door close, she exhaled a shaky breath. When she glanced back toward his room, only the tea service tray remained in the corridor.

"I AM SO very sorry Jon," said Phillip Madden, bracing an unsteady hand against the desk. "Yes, I understand. I will let him know right away." Hanging up the phone, he slowly turned his ashen face toward Richard.

"What is it? What happened?"

Hesitating, Phillip swallowed back the dryness in his throat. "I'm afraid I have some terrible news. It's about Oscar… he is… he has…" His voice failing him, he held Richard's eyes, and through his grave expression attempted to convey the tragic news.

Disbelief preceding acceptance of the seemingly impossible, Richard held his eyes briefly before his head collapsed into his hands.

"Jon found something in his car," said Phillip; the circumstances of Oscar's death, prompting him to speak after only a brief silence had passed. "A container."

Richard lifted his eyes.

"The contents of the container have tested positive for the same strain of *Mycobacterium bovis as infected the others.*"

"The contents?" Richard's voice cracked as he spoke.

"Manure."

Again Richard's head fell into his hands.

"He was at work when the symptoms presented. It was a night shift, skeleton crew. They must have panicked. The next morning Jon received a call. Arriving at the plant, he learned that at some point during the night, they had moved him into a storage closet." Pausing, Phillip swallowed hard. "That was were Jon found his body, on the floor of a storage closet."

SEARCHING RICHARD SINCLAIR'S eyes, Kate Mironov took hold of his trembling hands.

The genuine concern he saw in her gentle features stirred an upwelling of emotion he wasn't prepared for. Swallowing hard, he turned his face away and walked over to the desk.

Sitting down in the chair opposite, she waited for him to speak.

"What I wouldn't give for just an ounce of your strength right now," he said, speaking into his hands, held clasped in front of his mouth.

"My strength?"

"With everything you've been through," he said, his eyes meeting hers as they lifted over his hands. "How have you...? How do you...?"

"A duck treading water is a more accurate depiction of my coping skills. You know, you've seen it for yourself, my emotions are all over the place. Half the time, I'm just one determined blink away from breaking down in tears."

Tilting his head, he looked deep into her eyes. The hurt he now saw in their recesses reached deep into his heart. It was the kind of hurt one instinctively buries; the kind of hurt that seemed to mirror what he was feeling inside. He gently reached for her hand. Then, lightly pressing its warmth between his own, he held her eyes.

"Oh, I don't know," she said. "It's the little everyday things, like when I hear an ambulance siren or smell my mother's perfume; or when I see a father holding his little girl's hand. And you know that warning voice we're all born with?"

He nodded.

"Well, I no longer have that voice, not the way I used to. In the place of fear, a numbness has taken over, an indifference to my own well-being."

"But you know how important you are to me, to all of us."

Nodding, she lowered her eyes and stared down at their hands. "When the doctors first told me about my parents, I felt my world, my very existence, shatter into pieces. I remember being flooded with images I couldn't bear to look at. But no matter how tightly I closed my eyes, I couldn't escape them. At night I would turn up my music so loud it was impossible to think and still the images flashed through my mind: the times I disappointed them and that hurt look in dad's eyes when I—" She broke off, the rush of words now clogging her narrowing throat. Choking back a painful breath, she blinked away the sting of tears. She suddenly felt vulnerable and exposed, as though some protective seal had been broken and now the contents were spilling out for him to see.

He lowered his eyes. Partly, as it seemed the right thing to do, and partly, to conceal the guilt he was now feeling. Guilt for having failed to recognize such profound sadness in eyes incapable of deceit. He wondered at his insensitivity, his willingness to see only what he wanted to believe to be true. He wondered if there was something inherently missing from his make-up. Perhaps he was not so different from someone like Edward Blackwell after all. A chill passed over his skin.

"Hey," she said, tilting her head to meet his eyes. "I know what you're thinking and stop."

He turned his face away.

"We are the sum of our parts, no single experience or single trait defines us. You told me that once, remember? You are always so willing to see the worst in yourself that you overlook the strengths others see in you."

Slowly turning, he met her eyes, but did not speak.

"You had no way of knowing what was going on inside my head because I did not allow it to be known. I assumed people wanted to hear I was okay, and so I said I was okay. And after saying it enough times to others, I started to believe it myself. But it was false and hollow. And had it not been for your presence, your strength, your hand there to take hold of mine, I don't know how I would have made it through this."

He gently brushed the tears from her cheek. "You do know I am always here for you, right?"

"I know, and please don't look at me like that. I'm just working through the natural stages of grief. It's all perfectly normal."

"And what stage are you at now?"

"I seem to be stalled at anger."

"Should I be nervous?"

"Probably."

"Well, if you're stalled at anger, you certainly hide it well."

"The thing is Richard, we can only suppress our feelings for so long before they find a way to rise to the surface. And you don't want to end up like me, lashing out at those idiots who decide to stop and have a conversation at the bottom of escalators."

"I know you're right," he said, through a gentle laugh. "And I think you are the most amazing person I've ever met. Your presence in my life has given me the strength to confront twenty-two years' worth of self-doubt."

He could tell she wanted to speak, but didn't want to cry, and that the former would bring about the latter was certain. "Kate, I feel like I'm moving in slow-motion as everything speeds past me. So much has happened and is happening that I just need some time to get things clear in my own head first."

"I understand Richard. In fact, I probably understand better than most."

Nodding, he glanced up at the clock.

She followed his eyes. "I find it's best not to take on everything all at once."

"You're right," he said, breathing a heavy sigh.

"How about I leave you to finish up in here," she said, standing and reaching around him to collect her purse.

"Where are you going?"

"I'll go downstairs and work on the paper."

"You know, Alex was right about one thing."

"Alex? Oh, you mean about the phages."

"Well, yes, that, and about your being an absolute angel."

"Alex said that?"

"He did, and he was right."

THE OTHERS HAD already arrived by the time Adèle Leary stepped out of the shower. From her bedroom, she could hear the murmur of voices. Stepping back into her discarded jeans, she slipped a clean T-shirt over her head and walked out to the kitchen. Standing huddled around Jack, their expressions were grave as they looked down at a floor plan spread open across the kitchen table.

"They use the same design for each of their facilities. As you can see, it's basically a 4000 square foot warehouse, and that's no accident, the space is leased out for that purpose. There are two points of entry, the staff entrance at the side of the building and the loading dock at the back." Planting a finger down on the plan, Jack lowered his eyes. "This is where we will wait for Adèle's signal." Slowly lifting his eyes, he gave a cautioning glance around the table. "For obvious reasons they don't have surveillance cameras at the loading dock, but there are fixed position cameras at each corner of the building with a direct feed to Blackwell's private security company. Under no circumstances are you to remove your masks or speak our names aloud. I want us all to walk away from this free and in the clear." Pausing, he searched each face for any sign of reluctance.

"How are we going to get inside?" asked Mélanie, meeting his eyes directly.

Jack smiled, please his intuition had not failed him. "They use key cards. I have someone working on it. Rest assured it will be ready when we need it."

"Do you know when that will be?"

"We've only just managed to track him down, Annick. I will need some more time to follow his movements, not long, a week maybe two."

Catching Adèle's directed glance, he turned back to Stéphane. "And can I trust you to keep an eye on Henry?"

Stéphane gave him a firm nod.

"And if he resists?" added Adèle.

Turning, Stéphane held her eyes. "This is how it has to be," he said plainly. "Henry will realize that when the truth comes out."

CHAPTER TWENTY-FIVE

Exiting off the highway, Dr. Jon Monteiro cast a sidelong glance at Phillip Madden's solemn profile. "Two men, laborers from the feedlot, have been arrested."

Phillip's head swung around with such sudden force that for an instant, stars rained down over his eyes. "Arrested?"

"Saturday morning, at the airport, while attempting to board a flight to Brazil. They have confessed to selling manure from infected cattle to local farms. The feedlot has been shut down, and all employees placed under quarantine until the investigation is concluded.

Shaking his head, Phillip's features twisted in disgust. "Tell me Jon," he said, through a heavy sigh. "Help me to understand, what possible motivation is worth the price of a life?"

"As is often the case, money was the motivation. Though I agree, such actions are beyond comprehension."

"And the container, the one found in Oscar's car, is there any way of finding out where he got it from?"

"Some unwitting farmer, perhaps. We may never know for certain. Nor will we know why, given his suspicions, he didn't take the necessary precautions." Tightening his lips, Jon slowly shook his head. "If only he had discussed this with me beforehand."

"He would have known what you'd say Jon."

"But how can I not feel responsible?"

"By accepting that no one man can ever be held responsible for the actions of another."

A brief silence passed, before Phillip spoke again. "Is there any risk of ground contamination from run-off?"

Jon shook his head. "The manure is collected and sold commercially as organic fertilizer."

"Sold commercially? But that means we are dealing with a much larger geography in terms of potential exposure."

"Customs authorities have been alerted, though it is doubtful any contaminated material made it past their quality control."

"Doubtful?"

"Three months ago, while running their routine tests, the pathogen was detected in half a dozen cattle. The infected animals were immediately destroyed. Then, just over a month ago, it showed up again. This time, half of the herd was destroyed."

"Are they not mandated to report things like that?"

"Remember Phillip, this feedlot is part of Duluth-Crane's global operations. And if their actions are anything to go by, the only mandate they were given was to keep it contained and quiet."

"How the hell do you conceal the disappearance of that many head of cattle?"

"As before, they had the carcasses collected for incineration. However, this time the collection was done at night and the drivers were paid a hefty sum for their discretion. But unbeknownst to them, the Ministry had been tipped off."

"Tipped off?"

"The Director of Public Health had received an anonymous letter. The letter described the situation with the kind of detail only someone on the inside could have. The trucks were confiscated as soon as they left the lot and are now in quarantine as part of the investigation."

"So you're saying the Ministry knew about this, even as you were reporting to them about the outbreak. Why didn't they shut the operation down then and there? Surely, they must have made the connection."

"It's like I said before, Duluth-Crane. Understand Phillip, they would have needed something more substantial than a few permit violations to shut an operation like that down. The author of the letter would have had no way of knowing about the actions of the two arrested men at the time it was written. And considering how self-contained that lot was, the connection may not have been as obvious to them then, as it is to us now."

"Okay, so getting back to these arrests."

"The second time the pathogen showed up in their tests, the two men were again instructed to haul the manure away for disposal. However, this time, tragically, they saw an opportunity to make some extra cash, and did not dispose of all of it."

Shaking his head, Phillip's lips curled in disgust. "But working at the feedlot, they had to have known what they were exposing people to."

Pressing his lips, Jon slowly rocked his head. "I saw them on the news Phillip. I doubt very much they were capable of grasping the full consequences of their actions. They looked terrified, yes, but not in a guilty way, if you know what I mean. My guess is, the decision to leave the country was not one of their own choosing."

Phillip, undoubtedly more cynical than his friend, expressed as much in his features, but kept his thoughts to himself. "What's being done to keep this contained?"

"There is a ban on selling meat and produce in the markets until field tests are concluded."

"Field tests?"

Jon nodded. "Whether or not the Ministry only made the connection after I faxed them Richard's results, I cannot say; what I do know is, the next day, field officers were out collecting soil samples from farms in the vicinity of the feedlot."

Again, electing to keep his thoughts to himself, Phillip slowly turned his face toward the open window. Tepid air washed over his skin as his weary eyes followed the tawny transitions of the moving landscape. "Richard is making rapid progress," he said without turning. "That the phages have proven effective against the pathogen *in vitro* is promising."

"Promising is an understatement. I feel as though I've harnessed my own force of nature in that nephew of yours. His efforts will go a long way toward strengthening our case for funding when we meet with the Ministry tomorrow."

"In light of everything you've just told me—" Phillip broke off, his attention now distracted as they turned onto the rutted path leading to the clinic. "Surely they cannot all be here for vaccinations?"

"Unfortunately the Ministry has been swift to issue orders, but slow with their explanations. People are scared, frustrated and looking for answers."

RICHARD SINCLAIR STOOD in the doorway, propping it open, just slightly. Kate Mironov's eyes fell briefly upon the surgical mask, pulled down around his neck. Under the weight of his impatient stare, she suddenly felt very silly for her persistence, having percussed (whilst singing in her head) nearly two verses of *Waterfall* on the door before he finally threw it open.

"What is it Kate? I'm in the middle of something."

She waved her arm in front of him. "Notice anything different?"

His serious expression instantly softened. "Did they say if you'll need physiotherapy?"

"They said it is as good as new."

"It must feel good to finally have that off."

Holding his eyes, she nodded. "So, are you going to let me in?"

"Right now?"

"I have a few hours before my shift at the clinic and wanted to work on the paper."

Hesitating, he glanced over his shoulder and back at her.

"My shift at the clinic," she added with an ironic smile. "You know, the clinic, where I work assisting the vets with surgeries."

"That's not a fair comparison. You put things back together; I take them apart."

"I know your intentions are good, Richard, but I'm well aware of how this process works.

Lifting his chin, he considered for a moment. "Alright," he said, through a quiet sigh. "But just give me a few minutes to finish up." He then quickly stepped back behind the door.

CHAPTER TWENTY-SIX

The mood in the boardroom was austere. The expressions on the only two faces staring back at them were inscrutable. The others kept their heads down, busily making notes. Clearing his throat, the Director of Public Health, Manuel Almeida, stood up to speak. Phillip Madden lowered his eyes. In his head, he was readying himself for both the rejection of their proposal and the litany of excuses certain to precede it. Being of this mindset, it took some time for Manuel Almeida's words to register.

"*DID THAT JUST* happen?" Phillip Madden kept his voice low as they entered the lobby of the Health Ministry.

"I am certain there is a story behind it," said Dr. Jon Monteiro, "but frankly I am too relieved to question that right now."

Hearing his name, Phillip turned.

"Excellent, you are still here," said Manuel Almeida, pausing briefly to catch his breath. "I understand you will be seeing Edward Blackwell this afternoon?"

Phillip nodded.

Manuel handed him a sealed envelope. "Could you please ensure he receives this?"

"Certainly," said Phillip, bending down to place the envelope inside his briefcase.

With a nod, Manuel then turned and hurried back in the direction from which he had just come.

Jon stared down at the briefcase. "Do you think Edward may have had something to do with what just happened in there?"

Rolling his eyes, Phillip started to speak, then quickly changed his mind. "No," he said decisively. "I refuse to let him cast his shadow over this day."

GLIMPSING THE SMUG expression on Edward Blackwell's face, Phillip Madden's temples pulsated with indignation. "Here, you better give this to him," he said, removing the envelope from his briefcase and handing it to Jon. "I don't want to have to look at him if I can avoid it."

"Good afternoon, gentlemen," said Edward, stepping inside the back of the jeep. "I trust your meeting went well."

Clenching his jaw, Phillip fixed his eyes out the window, leaving Jon to relay the details of the Ministry's decision to Edward. He kept silent for the duration of the drive, tuning out their conversation with relative ease; that was, until he glimpsed Jon remove the envelope from the center console and pass it back to Edward.

NOW SEATED INSIDE one of the clinic's small examination rooms, Edward Blackwell felt as though the walls were closing in on him. Laboring to breathe, he unfastened the top button of his shirt collar. He cringed at the awareness of perspiration trickling down his back. Crossing his arms, he sat silent and with an eerie stillness, like some melting wax figurine.

During a brief break between patients, he stood up and addressed Dr. Jon Monteiro directly. "Would you mind if I borrowed your jeep for a couple of hours?"

Phillip's head shot up. "Why? Where are you going?"

Half-turning, Edward shot him an icy glance. "I would like to visit the settlement."

"What on earth for?"

"If you must know, I would like to get a better sense of the people who have been benefitting from my philanthropy."

"What? You mean the people you've been looking down your nose at for the past two hours."

"It is my understanding the settlement is under quarantine," said Jon, employing his most diplomatic tone.

Edward nodded slowly, holding Jon's eyes as he did so.

"And under the current circumstances, people are unlikely to be receptive to a stranger poking their nose around," added Phillip, his mind racing to determine both the motivation behind and potential consequences of this unexpected move.

"And yet you both felt it safe enough to send young Richard out there?"

"Even you must appreciate things have changed. Or am I wrong in assuming you were made aware one of your employees was the latest victim."

Edward looked between them through steely eyes. "With all due respect gentlemen, you appear to be under the misapprehension, I am seeking your permission. I am not. If you are intent upon making this difficult, I will simply have a car sent over from the plant."

Avoiding the challenge of Edward's eyes, Jon, preferring to be rid of him, reached into his pocket and handed him the keys.

"There, now that wasn't so difficult was it?" Turning, Edward slid the keys into his pocket and walked out the door.

"You are a more tolerant man than me my friend," said Jon, looking at Phillip with an empathetic frown. "I truly do not understand how you have managed to stay affiliated with him all these years."

"Let's just hope he invented that story as an elaborate ruse to relieve himself from staying here."

"Yes, I must admit he did not look at all well."

CLOSING THE DOOR behind him, James Sinclair sat down at his desk. For some time, he stared at the package in his hands. Its tangibility, a reminder of the man whose passing, he had not yet allowed himself to mourn. A reminder as well, of the life he had turned his back on all those years ago. He thought about how complicated everything had been back then. *If only Thomas could have seen what was before his eyes.*

Sliding the contents out onto his desk, he heard something clank. Picking up the wristwatch, he closed his eyes and held the leather band to his nose. Then, with trembling fingers, he removed his own watch, replacing it with Thomas's.

He looked through the assortment of flimsy gold-trimmed prize ribbons and faded academic certificates, each one stirring childhood memories long forgotten. There were bordered black and white photographs of him as a young child and of his mother with Thomas, the dates and locations of each written at the bottom in his mother's neat hand. He paused at a photograph of his father and Thomas, standing in front of an allied tank, smiling. His chest tightened with an eerie sadness when he looked at the date on the photograph—a moment captured in time. Three weeks later and his father would be killed, taken down by a sniper while pulling Thomas to safety. His head fell heavy in his hands. He cursed his father for his bravery, then immediately took it back. Lifting his eyes, he offered a silent apology to a man he had never really known; a conjured memory made real through photographs and stories.

Inside a small white envelope was a medal, a six pointed star attached to a red, white and blue ribbon. He turned it over in his hands. The initials of *King George VI* were stamped on the front. The back was blank. He held it to his cheek. Tears stung his eyes as he swallowed back the tightening in his throat.

Looking down at his desk, he noticed a folded note attached to the legal papers. He slid the note out from beneath the paper-clip. Closing his eyes, he drew a deep breath before opening it.

"My dearest James,

That my stubbornness has prevented me from knowing you as the husband, father and physician is a regret that weighs most heavily upon my conscience.
What is certain to me now, more than ever, is that I owe your family two debts of gratitude. The first is to your father, a man of incomparable courage, whose spirit, I know lives on in you. And the second is to both you and your mother, for your presence in my life gave it purpose and meaning at a time of my greatest despair.
You are the creation of two of the most extraordinary people I have ever known, and I am certain they would be proud of the man you have become.
The medal, the France and Germany Star, was awarded to your father posthumously. Your mother had placed it in my care

many years ago with the request it be passed down to you when the time was right. I have always kept it close to my heart, and it has given me courage throughout the years when I needed it most. I hope it will do the same for you.
May these brief, though heartfelt words guide you in your understanding of the decisions I have made in my Will.
I hope you live a life full of love and without regrets. Our time here on earth is far too short to be wasted.
I have loved you more than you will ever know. Thomas"

Swallowing and sniffling until he could barely breathe, James yielded to the heavy tears welling in his eyes, the sting and heat of each fading as they trailed down his cheeks. Taking a deep breath, he wiped them away with the back of his hand. Then, through watery eyes, he stared at the distorted black lettering on the page before him. Speaking the words in a whisper, he read aloud, "'*The Last Will and Testament of Thomas R. Blackwell.*'"

JOSEPH BORREGO TOOK his time to appraise the man now standing opposite him.

"I am afraid several people have tested positive as carriers of the infection," said Edward Blackwell, glancing up from the letter in his hand.

"Carriers?"

"My apologies, I assumed they had explained all this when they were out here. By carriers, I mean people who have tested positive for the infection but do not show symptoms. And though it is inactive inside them, it may still be transmitted to others."

"And they send you, a foreigner, to tell us this news."

"As you can appreciate, their resources have been stretched to the limit in dealing with this situation. And I, well, my company rather, has been working closely with the Health Ministry to develop a treatment for this illness. It is in that capacity they have sent me here today."

"May I see that list?"

Gently, Edward placed the letter in the hollow of Joseph's outstretched hand.

For some time Joseph's eyes travelled over the names, typed in bold black ink on the embossed Health Ministry letterhead.

Scratching thoughtfully at the white stubble on his chin, he carefully read through the lines of medical terminology typed beside each name. "What does all this mean?"

"We are not yet certain," said Edward, reaching into his pocket. "More testing still needs to be done. The Ministry sent me here today to provide each of those who tested positive with one of these tablets." In his hand he held out a plastic vial for Joseph to take. "They were developed by my company several years ago in response to a similar outbreak in Malawi.

Drawing his brow, Joseph stared down at the vial. "Medicine?"

"It prevents infections like this spreading from person to person, which, until a treatment becomes available, remains our primary objective."

Slowly lifting his eyes, Joseph studied Edward's face. He had grown weary of officials from the Ministry. Too many had descended upon them in recent days. "Okay," he said, breathing a reluctant sigh. "Leave it with me."

"They will each need to sign beside their name," said Edward, bending down to remove a folder from his briefcase.

"Why is this?"

"For the Ministry's records," said Edward, casually. "You will find a pen inside the folder."

An anxious hour passed before Edward saw a faltering blur approaching against the backdrop of the blinding afternoon sun. He breathed a relieved sigh.

Without speaking, Joseph handed him the folder and the empty vial.

Glancing quickly over the names, Edward then removed an envelope from the inside pocket of his linen suit jacket, and held it out between his fingers.

Eyeing the offered envelope, Joseph stood before him with arms crossed.

"Please," said Edward, softening his features into an expression of feigned compassion. "Consider it a small token of the Ministry's appreciation for your continued cooperation."

JAMES SINCLAIR TURNED when Abby entered.

"I brought you some tea," she said, setting the cup down on the corner of the desk.

"You had better have a seat," he said, his eyes now fixed on the page in front of him.

When she was seated, he began to read aloud:

"'With all net revenue received from the sale of my shares to be deposited into The Blackwell Foundation account, herein specified; and from which proceeds are to be drawn upon and dispersed, exclusively for the purpose of philanthropic endeavors chosen at the sole discretion and under the sole authorization of James J. Sinclair.'"

He lifted his eyes. "The rest is about the administration and operation of the *Foundation* itself, amounts to be dispersed per annum and so forth."

Abby was silent.

"This decision only affects Thomas' shares," said James, reading the thoughts behind her troubled expression. "Edward has more than enough of his own money."

She swallowed to ease the sharp pain in her throat. "So what are you going to do?"

"How could I deny him his last wish after everything he did for my mother and me?"

"I understand that James, but do you not think Edward is going to try to fight this?"

"There's a no-contest clause."

"But what would he have to lose?"

"There are other assets to which he is the sole beneficiary, properties here and overseas."

Abby fought hard to suppress her emotions, nodding mechanically as her thoughts crept back to that day, that darkest of days, when she had found herself an object to which Edward had felt himself entitled.

"As per his wishes, his ashes have been interred in the family crypt. A memorial is being held on Monday evening."

"Perhaps it is best if you go on your own."

James reached across the desk for her hand. "I'm not sure I can do this without you by my side."

"But what if he tries something?"

"He wouldn't dare."

"Are you sure about that?"

"I am certain."

"And what about Henry and Richard? How are we going to explain all this to them?"

"There's no point in saying anything until we have confirmed all the details."

SOMETHING DIDN'T FEEL right. His instincts alerted, Edward Blackwell stood hesitant. Removing the folded paper from his jacket pocket, he glanced down at the deceased's name, *Maria Tregeira*; his eyes, then moved across to the names likely to be seeking compensation on her behalf. Refolding the paper, he tucked it back inside his pocket and deliberated. He kicked at some loose stones until finally coaxed forward by the dual annoyances of dust covered shoes and indecision.

After passing several overturned oil drums and debris tossed about by the wind, he stood in front of a plywood door, lightly tapping his knuckles against its rough surface.

Just as he was turning to leave, he heard a scraping noise and glanced back. He blinked as the withered figure stepped into the light, his translucent skin and rheumy eyes lending him the appearance of the dead brought back to life.

Introducing himself as an official from the Health Ministry, Edward attempted to explain the reason for his visit in his fractured Portuguese. Whether or not the man understood any of what he had said was unclear, as he made no reply. Rather, his thin, jagged lips twisted into a smile of sorts as he slowly turned, motioning for Edward to follow.

Stepping inside, the stench of perspiration and sickness quickly overwhelmed his senses. It took his eyes a few seconds to adjust to the darkness. The single lit kerosene lamp suspended from the ceiling was doing little to illuminate the room. He drew back at the sight of a woman lying on a sheet on the earthen floor. A pile of blood stained rags was heaped next to her shivering body. Kneeling at her side, a young girl was applying a wet cloth to her forehead.

As his eyes lifted, they were drawn toward a young man seated in the far corner of the room. He looked catatonic, his body swaying to some rhythm only he could hear. Edward stumbled back, almost losing his balance when the rocking abruptly stopped and the man's vacant eyes fixed upon him directly. Turning back to the old man, Edward, using more silent gesture than words, asked what had happened. Lifting his withered hand, the old man pointed to a tiny bundle, wrapped in white cloth.

No sooner had Edward glimpsed the tiny white bundle, than panic overtook his senses. His eyes darted between the blank faces in the room, motioning for them to help. When no one moved, he dropped his briefcase and hurried toward the woman. He knelt down opposite the young girl and searched her eyes for approval before reaching across and feeling for the woman's pulse. It was weak.

Barely conscious, her feverish skin was drenched with perspiration. Suddenly, her weakened body began convulsing. He grabbed hold of her shoulders, bracing her head as it thrashed against the earthen floor. And then, just as suddenly as it had begun, the shaking stopped and her limp, lifeless body draped motionless in his arms.

The room began to spin. He felt his grip on reality slipping away, but was powerless to stop it. He blinked. And when he opened his eyes, it was as though his consciousness had divided, with one pristine version of himself looking across at the other, now tainted and trapped inside this nightmarish canvass. He could sense the baby's presence in the room. Its innocent soul juxtaposed with his own, so long past redemption. He could hear his father's voice, stern and laden with disappointment, directing him to look around the room, to look upon the true face of suffering. He was delirious.

When Edward regained his senses, the elderly man stepped away from him. In his frail hand he held the cool wet cloth that had been used to revive him. Edward shook his head. The motion sent a shock wave of pain coursing through his skull and down his neck. He closed his eyes until the flashes of light dissipated.

Slowly lifting his lids, he saw that the young girl was no longer kneeling beside the woman, and that a white sheet had been placed over the body. He stared down at the sheet for some time. And the longer he stared, the more it came to seem plausible that through holding her in his arms as she had passed, she had relieved him of his suffering, carried his sins away with her to heaven.

When he felt his equilibrium restored, he attempted to stand. Then, slowly sweeping his eyes across the room, three names flashed through his mind: The first, lay dead on the floor before him; the second, sat slumped over in the corner chair, inconsolable; and the third, stood staring into his withered palms, as though searching for answers in their crisscrossing lines. He quickly calculated the eventuality of how this might all play out in the clear light of day, when grief turned to anger and anger to retribution. He measured the weight of the signatures he had already obtained against any future claim these two might attempt to make. And then, with a nod perceived by no one, he picked up his briefcase, walked toward the door and quickly exited the home.

"PLEASE TELL ME you are calling with good news."
"And hello to you, too."
"Sorry, uncle, I'm having a bad day."
"Something we need to discuss?"
"No, just the usual."
"I do have some news to share, if you're up for it."
"I'm all ears."
"The samples the Ministry collected have tested negative."
"So we can confidently rule out latent carriers."
"Correct, which will go a long way toward keeping this contained."
"And I take it from your tone the meeting went well."
"They've agreed to foot the bill for everything."
"But how will that work?"
"Can you not recognize good news when you hear it?"
"Yes, no, I mean, yes, this is fantastic news, of course."
"Richard, so much has happened, I don't know where to begin."
Richard Sinclair listened as Phillip Madden recounted the details of the feedlot closure, and its links to the initial outbreak. When he finished speaking the line was silent.
"Richard did you get all that?"
"Yes, sorry, it's just hard not to think if only…"
"You are thinking about Oscar?"
Again, the line went silent.
"Richard?"
"Yes, I'm here."

"Are you okay?"

"I'm fine."

"I expect the deal should go through by Friday, and then I will speak to Edward. Mind you, I will probably hold off until the flight back home so he can no longer inflict any damage over here."

"Why? What has he done?"

"It's nothing I can't handle."

Another brief silence passed.

"Perhaps we should leave it there for now."

"There's just one thing, and well, it actually reinforces how important it is they are ready to mobilize should another outbreak occur."

"Why? What have you found?"

"I'm seeing a marked decrease in the efficacy of the phages when administered four hours after the initial infection; to the point where after twelve hours, its therapeutic effect becomes negligible."

"Any theories as to why?"

"Tissue culture results strongly suggest the phages are unable to cross the cell membrane; meaning, it is only by first infecting pathogen present outside the cells that they can then be transported across the membrane. What I'm thinking is, as time progresses and the infection spreads, the concentration of extracellular pathogen decreases to the point where it can no longer function as an efficient transporter."

"So we are dealing with a very narrow window."

"For now at least, yes, that does seem to be the case."

CHAPTER TWENTY-SEVEN

Violet-gray slivers of pre-dawn light crept through the heavy curtains of Phillip Madden's hotel room. His groggy morning voice unable to articulate anything beyond a grunt, he sat on the edge of his unmade bed with his bleary eyes fixed questioningly upon Dr. Jon Monteiro, wondering at the reason behind his early morning wake-up call.

Having yet to speak, the only movement in Jon's grave expression was the shifting of his bloodshot eyes, their puffy lids drooping under the weight of their fatigue. Pouring two cups of coffee, he handed one to Phillip and nodded toward the front page of the newspaper. "There has been a new development," he said, keeping his voice low, as though to ease his imposition upon the silence.

Shifting his drowsy eyes, Phillip glanced down at the photograph.

"Below the photo," continued Jon, "is a statement from Duluth-Crane. It seems they are attempting to shift the burden of responsibility for the outbreak onto EBP."

Suddenly alert, Phillip's head shot up. "EBP? You mean Edward's Company? But I thought the source had been traced to the cattle at the feedlot."

"It has, but Duluth is accusing EBP of having caused the cattle to become infected in the first place." Pausing briefly, Jon lifted the coffee cup to his lips. "In their statement, they say how EBP

140

was awarded the contract to supply feed supplements for their global feedlot operations; feed supplements which were to have included antibiotics." He held his raised brow in an arch, as though he had anticipated a less sedate reaction to his words.

"Go on," said Phillip, his voice the cautious tenor of one hearing unsettling news before their fatigued mind can fully process its implications.

"Typically, how this works is they will supplement the feed with a sub-therapeutic dose of antibiotics, just enough to promote growth in the cattle and prevent the spread of disease. However, if not strictly regulated, this practice has the potential to create an environment where bacteria can become tolerant to the continuous presence of low dose antibiotics. Add to that the chance occurrence of a lethal strain developing, and you now run the risk of spreading these lethal and antibiotic resistant bacteria into the human population."

"Huh," grunted Phillip, running his hands across his brow. "He was right to think the plant was somehow involved."

"Richard?"

"His original theory was that leaked waste from the reservoir had contaminated the waterways. And that the use of this water for irrigation had, over time altered the microbes present in the soil."

"A theory which by its very plausibility should serve as a caution to be heeded. And one which must, as all theories must, evolve with the evidence."

A few seconds passed before Phillip drew in his chin and gave his head a decisive shake. "Although I am hardly inclined to rise to Edward's defense, it seems clear to me that through their decision to conceal evidence, it is the feedlot, or rather Duluth, who ultimately bear responsibility for what happened."

"Ah yes, but Duluth is accusing EBP of deliberately diluting the concentration of antibiotics in their feed supplements in order to turn a larger profit, in essence adding fuel to the fire."

"And they can prove this claim?"

"Someone has come forward with evidence, internal correspondence and directives to alter protocols."

Setting his coffee cup down on the bed, Phillip took his head in hands. "Global operations," he said, speaking through his fingers, "you said EBP was given the contract for Duluth's global feedlot operations?"

"It is possible EBP only altered the concentrations for select feedlots, lower profile sites they assumed would have less stringent controls in place. Perhaps they were just testing the waters to see if they could get away with it."

"Crooks, the lot of them," spat Phillip.

Nodding, Jon's agreement was groaned through a heavy sigh.

"And what does all this mean for Edward?"

"I imagine the authorities will want to speak with him; that is, if they have not already."

"But this makes no sense. He had to have known about this before coming over here."

"Corporate battles fought in print only ever provide contrived versions of actual events. If I were to speculate, I would say he was given reason to believe himself protected."

"And the Ministry, do you think this development has anything to do with their decision to green-light our proposal?"

"The optics do lend to that impression, yes."

"What do you suppose was in that envelope Manuel Almeida gave him?"

"It may have been a copy of the evidence they have against him."

"Is Manuel the kind of man who would do something like that?"

"Every man has his price."

"That sounds like something Edward would say."

"Sadly, there is a reason why men like Edward manage to survive as long as they do."

"The Edward I know is incapable of owning up to his mistakes, but if he does feel at all threatened by these claims, I have no doubt he will do whatever it takes to save his own skin."

"Go and have your shower," said Jon, reaching for the phone. "I will make the arrangements for the next flight out."

BUTTONING UP HIS dress shirt, Phillip Madden poked his head out the bathroom door. The room was empty. Spotting the note, he walked toward the bed and picked it up.

"I rebooked your flight out of Maputo for 1:00 p.m. today. See you shortly. Jon"

He drew back at the sudden knock on the door. It had an impatient, authoritative quality, and for a second panic rendered him motionless.

"Phillip, it's me."

Exhaling his relief, Phillip hurried toward the door.

"Edward's been taken into custody," blurted Dr. Jon Monteiro, the words escaping between gasping breaths.

"What?"

"There was a great commotion in the lobby."

"Taken into custody? Does that mean he has been arrested?"

"I'm not sure. The officers were leading him out the door as I entered. He called out for me to contact Manuel Almeida."

"You better make the call," said Phillip, speaking through a heavy sigh as he sunk down onto the bed.

Jon dialed through to Manuel Almeida's office. A few seconds of silent nodding followed his hurried words. Lowering the phone from his ear, he held Phillip's eyes, but did not speak.

"What did he say?"

"He said the situation had escalated beyond his ability to exert any influence over it."

"That's it?"

Tightening his lips, Jon rocked his head. "I don't know Phillip. It was strange. I could hear the fear in his voice."

"Fear of what might come out if Edward is backed into a corner."

"Self-preservation is indeed a great motivating force." Jon glanced at his watch. "Listen Phillip, it is still early, but I would feel better getting you over to the airport, just in case."

"And Edward?"

"How that all plays out is beyond our control. I will get word to Richard if anything develops."

LUCIDITY BE DAMNED, Phillip Madden thought to himself, washing back two sleeping pills with a glass of single malt. The hours passed slowly as he sat at the airport bar with his eyes glued to the departures board, watching and waiting, his consciousness fading.

No sooner had he collapsed into his seat on the plane, than he was snoring like a bear. And although he would awake a few hours later with an excruciating headache, he would not once chide himself for his indulgence, for it had afforded him what he craved most in that moment: a temporary escape from reality.

CHAPTER TWENTY-EIGHT

Although he was at a loss to explain how exactly, he was certain the scene with which his eyes were now met had in some way been altered. Locking his office door behind him, Phillip Madden set his briefcase down on the floor. Stepping forward, his movements were cautious as he waded through the impressionistic residue of the intruder's wake. Edging behind his desk, he brushed the books on the shelf to the side and slid open the wood paneling. The door of the safe swung open. Slumping back against his desk, his thoughts were muttered beneath his breath.

Dragging a chair over to the far corner of the room, he removed the cassette from the security camera and slid it into the VCR. He then watched the grainy image of a masked figure entering his office, standing on the edge of a chair and smearing something over the camera lens. It was impossible to make out the details of what happened next, but after a few minutes, a distorted figure could be seen scurrying back toward the door.

The ringing phone startled him. He answered with a grunt. The sound of Richard's muted chuckle made him smile, if only slightly.

"I take it you got Jon's message."

"You mean about Edward? I can't say I'm surprised."

"Do you think his lawyers have delayed telling him about the sale going through?"

"I think we can safely assume he's aware of our plans."

"What are we going to do if he comes here?"

"He won't."

"Are you sure?"

"I'm certain. In fact, I imagine right about now he's holed up in his hotel room emptying the contents of the bar fridge."

"Huh?"

"His father's memorial is today."

Richard was silent.

"Was there something else?"

"I just got off the phone with Dr. Halperin. She's faxed over the sequencing results."

"Did they turn up anything interesting?"

"Interesting, yes, though not entirely unexpected."

"*Mycobacterium bovis?*"

"Correct. She found mutations in two regulatory genes. One, involved in cell growth, and the other in the cell wall's response to environmental stimuli. She said they recently sequenced a strain with similar mutations, isolated from soil samples collected in Chile."

"Chile? Was she not more specific?"

"I'm afraid not. I could tell she was reluctant to speak with me."

"Would you mind faxing what she sent over to Jon's office at the hospital?"

"All of it?"

"Just her summary, I'll call him later to explain. First, I need to find out more about these Chilean soil samples.

"You're thinking this may be connected to Duluth?"

"Leave it with me for now. I'll call you after I've had a chance to speak with Rachel."

THOUGH HIS INTERNAL monologue was conjuring up every possible combination of expletive and derogatory Irish stereotype he could think of, Henry Sinclair sat stony-faced, watching as Jack Doherty paced the floor in front of him. The theatrics went on for some time, with Jack wringing his hands through heavy sighs, as though resigning himself to the telling of some unfortunate truth. Stopping abruptly, he fixed Henry with a cryptic gaze. He then reached into his pocket, removed a cigarette from the pack, and began threading it through his long, slender fingers like a coin.

"You know Henry, there was a time when I trusted you. But

then, well, let's just say I've been given good reason to doubt your loyalty."

"You're kidding, right? Is that why you called me here? I never breathed one word about what we saw that night at VNP, not to my family, not to anyone." Slamming his hands down on the desk, he jumped to his feet and started toward the door.

With his back turned, two hands suddenly landed on his shoulders. Reeling around, he looked up into Stéphane's unyielding face. It was a face he had known for years, and yet, it now seemed almost unrecognizable. His warm eyes had turned cold and were peering down at him, challenging him to make another move.

Henry quickly calculated his options. There was no way he could physically overpower Stéphane. He glanced over his shoulder at the path to the door, with a quick sprint he would be out in seconds. He just needed to wait for the exact instant when he could make his move. Shifting his eyes so as not to draw attention to his thoughts, he cast a look of exasperation toward Adèle. She met his eyes with a chilly smile. It was the sort of smile he had not known her capable of expressing. He turned toward the sound of Jack's voice.

"Sorry Henry, but I am afraid you're not going anywhere. You need to hear what I have to say."

"Jack, are you out of your mind? There are still people in the halls. If you don't let me go, I swear to god I'll…"

"You'll what, Henry? Scream?" Jack's head fell back in a cackle. "We both know that's not going to happen, but it'd almost be worth it to see you try."

"So what's the plan, Jack? Even you must realize you can't keep me here against my will."

With his head lowered and his hands joined behind his back, Jack approached. "Your uncle is a partner at Blackwell Laboratories, and as you know Edward—"

"This? Again? Are you serious?"

Raising his hand as though to quiet an unruly child, Jack gently motioned for silence. "But you're right Henry, I am getting off track." He cast his eyes toward the ceiling. "You are familiar with the group I was involved with back home?"

Henry was silent.

"Yes, well, as you can appreciate, our success in shutting down those breeding operations created a wee bit of inconvenience for a market in need of a continuous supply of animals for their research. Some in the industry got a little nervous. If it could happen in the UK, then where next? Though not the sort to be deterred by a wee bit of inconvenience, an alternative plan was hastily devised; a safety net, so to speak. But in order to successfully execute their plan, they needed the assistance of people with knowledge of how to maneuver through the loopholes. People with deep pockets, influence and perhaps most importantly, people unburdened by scruples. The sort of privileged scum who'd be attracted to the very simplicity of the plan's depravity."

"What the hell does any of this have to with me?"

"Guilt by familial association, I'm afraid. You see Henry, Edward Blackwell belongs to a network of shall we say, like minded opportunists; a group comprised of the sort who, like him, believe themselves entitled to act on their whims with impunity; and sadly, as you have seen for yourself, all too often that is the case."

"I was as disturbed by what I saw at VNP as you were, but seriously Jack, a network of privilege? You know what this sounds like, right?"

"Conspiracies to mask conspiracies," said Jack, his widening grin revealing a row of jagged nicotine stained teeth. "The truth of any deception can always be traced to the basest of human attributes. The rest is smoke and mirrors; speculation, floated into the ether to make the truth seem less plausible. It has always been this way. A network of powerful people, sitting atop the pyramid of humanity and pulling the strings. You can call them by whatever name you want. They are empowered by the skepticism of people like you Henry. They thrive from our very reluctance to believe in their existence. But you see, all we have to do is expose the truth. Reveal it in such a way that its existence can no longer be denied. And if we can manage to bring one down, then we will weaken the foundation of the entire network. The time has come to exploit the very weakness that gives them their strength."

"And how exactly do you intend to pull that off?"

"Ah," sighed Jack, looking back at him with a crooked smile. "The primary instinct of people like Edward Blackwell is to act first and foremost in the interest of self-preservation. The survival of the others will depend upon their distancing themselves from him when he is exposed."

"But if what you say is true, then aren't they just as much to blame as him?"

"What happens to them is out of my hands. My assignment is Edward Blackwell, others will handle the rest."

"Your assignment? Others?"

"Can you seriously not see where all this is going? Think for a minute Henry. Think about what I've said. Think about what you've seen. Think about that lovely new animal shelter where your friend works; and think about the dozens more like it that have sprung up across *Québec*."

Henry's head jerked back as the delayed realization struck him with blunt force. "They're using the animals from shelters?"

Jack nodded.

"But... but how is that even possible?"

"Perhaps that is a question better answered by your friend."

"There's no way she knows anything about this."

"Either way, the fact remains, the scheme's success hinged upon the willingness of the staff at these shelters to turn a blind eye to what was going on around them."

"But this doesn't make any sense. Suppliers here haven't been shut down. If what you say is true, then what the hell are they using the animals for?"

"Come now Henry, surely you can't be that thick." Pausing, he tightened his lips and held Henry's bewildered eyes. "The thing is Henry, what we have planned is too important to risk leaving any loose ends. And the question of your loyalty risks compromising plans that have been years in the making. I really wish it didn't have to be this way. Unfortunately, we all carry with us the burdens of our relations."

Looking between them, Henry tried to estimate the lengths they would be willing to go to expose something like this. He swallowed. His mind was racing. And then, suddenly aware of the loosened grip on his arm, he wrenched it free and made a desperate dash toward the door.

His chin took the brunt of the impact, crashing down hard onto the concrete floor. And now, after having been forced to his feet by

Stéphane, he stood glaring at Jack through defiant eyes, both pain and pride stopping him from voicing the question on his tongue.

A deliberate smirk bent the corners of Jack's thin red lips. "Because, Henry, we all have our part to play in what happens tonight." Exchanging a look with Stéphane, he then motioned for Adèle to follow as he walked out the door.

HENRY SINCLAIR HAD never had the need to size up Stéphane Brunot before, and now that he did, his eyes kept fixing on the size of his massive hands. Though their personalities had never truly meshed, they did still share a history. He thought back to the summer Stéphane had come to stay with his family after his mother had passed away, and in the middle of that thought, he said aloud, "Have you forgotten all that?"

His words were met with a blank expression. Henry stared into his large saucer of a face. A shadow had been cast over the warm amber eyes. Every trace of the gentleness in his features was now absent, replaced by a resolute coldness.

His blood flow partially cut off by the tightly bound ligatures, Henry shifted to release the tension in his limbs. The movement drew Stéphane's attention and he gave Henry a cautioning stare.

"Circulation," said Henry. "You've cut off my circulation." Forcing an easy laugh, he added, "You keep this up much longer, and you will have destroyed my aspirations for the NFL."

Stéphane grunted a mirthless chuckle.

"Seriously Stéphane, how long have we known each other?"

"I'd say about six years," he replied, his tone neutral.

"Six years, you do still remember that day, right? And what would have happened if my parents hadn't been there to intervene." Pausing, he searched the amber eyes for any sign of softening, but found none. "Stéphane, you know Jack will sell you out in a heartbeat if he gets pulled in for this, right?"

"You don't even know what he's got planned."

"What I do know, is right now you still have a chance to do the right thing."

"I appreciate your concern Henry, but I think it's best I stick to the plan."

"Please Stéphane, just tell him someone came to the door and started asking questions."

"And what will you do if I let you go?"

Henry was silent.

"Yeah, I thought as much." Sliding off the desk, Stéphane reached into his pocket for a roll of duct tape. Tearing a piece off, he brushed it across Henry's mouth. "I've got to go make a call. Just sit tight, it won't be much longer."

USING THE TIPS of his toes and all of the energy he could muster, Henry Sinclair inched the chair toward the door. After several agonizing seconds he had reached it. Drenched in sweat, his heart pounding in his chest, he tried to kick at the door with his toes, but there wasn't enough give. Shifting the chair sideways, he stretched out his elbow and started thrashing it against the door. He froze at the sound of someone jiggling the locked handle.

"Hello... Hello, is someone in there?"

Hearing the female voice, he called out for help; the desperation in his pleading wail was amplified in its effect by the tape covering his mouth.

"It's going to be okay," she said, placing her cheek against the door. "My name is Sophie, and I'm going to go get help."

Brushing past Stéphane as he stepped off the escalator, Sophie stopped and turned. "Hey," she called out, her voice shrill with panic as she pointed toward the door.

He turned, cautiously.

"Someone's locked inside that room. It sounds like they've had a stroke or something. Could you wait by the door in case one of the custodians comes by?"

Nodding, Stéphane turned back and slowly walked toward the door of room 306. As soon as she was out of sight, he darted toward the fire exit.

"HELP IS COMING, " said Sophie, pressing her ear against the door. "We'll have you out of there soon."

A few minutes later an elderly man in a brown maintenance uniform stepped off the escalator. His casual expression and unhurried pace made clear the urgency of her message had not been relayed. In his right hand, a massive key ring swayed back and forth as though to the rhythm of some tune in his head.

"Sylvain," she called out, noticing the name embroidered on his shirt pocket. "Please hurry, I think he may be injured."

After fumbling with the dozens of keys on the ring for the correct one, Sylvain finally managed to unlock the door.

Sophie pushed past him. Removing the tape from Henry Sinclair's mouth, she held his eyes—her own wide with panic.

"Please, we don't have much time," he gasped. "We need to call the police."

"What do I tell them?" she said, shock lending an unnatural calm to her voice.

"The people who did this to me are on their way to the animal shelter in NDG" Gulping back another breath, he quickly added, "And they may have a hostage."

Now trembling and a ghostly shade of white, Sylvain crouched down to cut the ties from Henry's ankles. As both men slowly rose to their feet, Sylvain's glassy eyes shifted with concern between the bruises on Henry's wrists and the cut on his chin.

"I'll be fine," said Henry, bracing himself against the chair at the sudden rush of blood to his limbs. "But you should probably go. Trust me, no one will be the wiser, and there's no need to involve yourself in this mess."

"DID YOU SPEAK to the police?"

Nodding, Sophie paused to catch her breath. "They're sending someone over to check it out. I didn't mention what happened here, just that it was something I had overheard."

"Thank you," said Henry, vaguely recalling her name but not certain enough to say it aloud.

Her sympathetic features were marked with concern as she looked him over. "Do you need me to take you to the hospital?"

He held her eyes, as he shook his head; though behind his own, his mind was racing. "I need to get to a phone."

Hearing his brother's voice, Henry Sinclair exhaled his relief. "Is Kate there with you?"

"Yes."

"And Uncle Phillip?"

"He's here too."

"Thank god, and you're all okay?"

"Yes. Did the police reach you at home?"

"The police?"

"So wait a minute, you're not at home?"

"No. Please, just tell me what happened."

"A suspicious package was delivered to the lab, and the police said someone had called in some kind of threat."

"Threat?"

"I don't know the specifics, Uncle Phillip insisted they talk to him in private."

"Are the police still there?"

"One officer is staying."

"What was in the package?"

"Just some firecrackers, rigged to go off when they opened the lid. Uncle Phillip said it was all just some kind of prank, but someone sure went through a lot of effort for a prank. Officers from the bomb disposal unit were here. They're heading over to the house now."

"The house?"

"They received another call about a package having been left at our house. We've been trying to track you down. Where are you?"

"Did you tell the police about Walter?"

"Walter will be fine. We were just heading home when I heard the phone ring, and something made me think it might be you."

"Do they know who called in these threats?"

"I'm not sure. Like I said, I'm getting all my information filtered through Uncle Phillip."

Henry was silent as his mind searched for some connection between Jack's words, and what Richard was now telling him.

"Henry, what's going on? Where are you right now?"

"I think this may all just be some kind of diversion."

"A Diversion? A diversion for what?"

"All I know for certain is it involves Edward Blackwell and the animal shelter. Beyond that, I have no idea."

"The shelter?" said Richard, casting a questioning glance toward Kate, who was waiting for him by the door.

"Yes. I will explain everything when I see you."

"Have you called the police?"

"They're on their way to the shelter now."

"I wish you would just tell me what's going on, Henry."

"I honestly don't know. I thought I had him pegged, but after tonight I don't know what he might be capable of."

"You still haven't told me where you are."

"I'll be home soon. There's just one more thing I need to do first."

Hanging up the phone, Henry sunk to the floor and tucked his head into his folded legs. Hearing someone approach he lifted his eyes.

"Here, please take this," said Sophie, holding out a bottle of water.

Struggling to his feet, he met her dark eyes with an awkward smile.

"It's Henry, right?"

He nodded, searching to recall her name.

"It's Sophie, I'm in your economics class."

"Ah yes, that's right," he said, nodding; though he sensed she could tell he was lying. "I was beginning to think people like you didn't exist."

"Oh, but we do exist, I can assure you. We lurk in the shadows, lying in wait to come to the aid of economics students in distress."

With a faint smile, he held her eyes, twice hesitating as he opened his mouth to speak.

"The police should be there by now," she said, guessing at what he was thinking. "Are you sure you want to go?"

Pulling his brow, he gave her a questioning smile.

"All that lurking about in the shadows makes one adept at reading people."

"I just need to know that everything's okay. I need to see it with my own eyes."

"Come on then," she said, motioning toward the escalator with a tilt of her head. "We can take my car."

CHAPTER TWENTY-NINE

"You're early. No matter. Get undressed."

Panic rendered Adèle Leary motionless. The sight of Edward Blackwell in his bathrobe brought with it a flood of nightmarish visualizations. Cradling a glass in his hand, he took a lingering sip while running his eyes over her appraisingly. She could tell from the fierce glint in his scrutinizing stare, the experience he had in store for her was certain to be unpleasant. The instant he turned to top up his glass, she sprang for the door.

"Good evening, Mr. Blackwell."

Edward spun around, sending his drink sloshing over the edge of the glass. Setting it down, his eyes narrowed and shifted between them as he steadied his feet to stand his ground. Taking measure of the lanky figure now stood before him, he saw an expression of derision equal to any he himself could muster. Nevertheless, being a man, who, by his very nature was resistant to the effects of intimidation, he responded to the intruders with a composed demeanor and a sympathetic smirk. "I should have known straight away from the looks of her something wasn't right. But you see," he lifted a hand to his chest, "I am not a man without compassion." Turning back toward the desk, he reached for his wallet. "So what is it you're after, money, credit cards?"

Suddenly, the wind was knocked from his lungs as Jack Doherty tackled him onto the bed.

"Now!" shouted Jack, his knees digging into Edward's gut as he struggled to hold back his flailing arms.

Grabbing the syringe from her coat pocket, Adèle flicked the cover off the needle and plunged it into Edward's leg. Anxious seconds passed before the sedative took effect. Soon he was unconscious.

Quickly changing out of his thrift shop suit, Jack grinned to himself as he proceeded to pull the musty tweed fabric over Edward's pliable limbs.

Adèle, having moments prior raced down the stairs to the room Jack had reserved, now stepped off the elevator on the fourteenth floor, pushing an empty wheelchair.

"You better get him downstairs," said Jack, lifting Edward into the chair. "Go to the back exit. I'll be waiting for you there."

Standing in a cold sweat, Adèle could barely manage the rhythm of her breath as she waited for the elevator to arrive. Nervously biting at her thumbnail, she kept glancing over her shoulder as every worst case scenario played out in her head. When the doors finally opened, she released her breath and quickly pushed the wheelchair inside, angling her back to the door should anyone else enter on the way down.

Idling in the alleyway behind the hotel, the rusted-out black van Jack had managed to procure was coughing up noxious clouds of dark gray smoke into the crisp night air. Above its congested tail pipe, a pair of heavy doors hung perilously askew on broken hinges. Exchanging an adrenaline fueled glance, they quickly lifted Edward's limp body inside. Then, maneuvering the back doors into alignment, they closed them with a quick, forceful push and sprinted to the front of the van.

CATCHING HER REFLECTION in the window as they passed beneath a street light, Adèle Leary removed the blond wig, kicked off her heels, and reached into her backpack for her jeans and sneakers. The billboards and lights blurred and streaked as she stared vacantly out the window. The blind devotion one in love recklessly places in the object of their affection had carried her this far. But now, seated next to him in the particular kind of stillness and silence that follows an initial rush of adrenaline, she could hear her warning voice sounding its alarm. Her stomach tightened and twisted as the reality of what they had just done permeated her consciousness. Casting a sidelong glance at Jack, she searched for traces of uncertainty, but saw none. With her head resting against the window, she wrestled her intuition into submission and gradually summoned up the courage to see the night through.

Enraged groans and a string of grumbled profanities preceded Edward Blackwell's ability to organize his thoughts into words. "Where am I?" he growled, jerking his body upright in an awkward flailing motion, the sudden movement causing him to writhe in spasms of pain.

"You'd be wise to lay back and keep quiet. I imagine you're going to have one hell of a headache," said Jack, glancing into the rear view mirror with a pitiless smirk.

Turning off the headlights, Jack drove to the warehouse in the back of the animal shelter and parked alongside a ravine, bordering the lot.

The beam from a flashlight caught Adèle's eye. "That must be them, over there, by the loading dock."

"Good, then they are in position."

They turned toward the headlights of a white cube van now entering the parking lot. Grabbing the masks from the dashboard, they pushed open their doors and hurried toward the back of the van. Climbing inside, Jack tore off a piece of duct tape and brushed it over Edward's mouth. "And should you have any doubt about my willingness to use this," he said, removing a pistol from his backpack, "just remember, that at this point I've got nothing left to lose."

Taking hold of Edward's arm, Jack forced him across the gravel lot to where Mélanie and Annick were waiting. Veering left, Adèle kept low as she hurried along the forested perimeter toward the staff entrance to the warehouse.

Now crouched down low, and with their pointed grips dug firmly into Edward's defiant limbs, Mélanie and Annick watched through wide and flashing eyes as Jack edged along the side of the cube van.

Pausing only for the instant it took him to glance in the side mirror and see the door was unlocked, Jack lurched forward and pulled on the handle. Both cheeseburger and clipboard fell from the stunned driver's stubby fingers as his hands shot up. Jack motioned with the pistol for him to step out of the van. He then quickly fastened his fleshy wrists together and fixed a piece of duct tape over his food stained mouth.

Tugging a reluctant cargo, Mélanie and Annick hurried toward the loading dock. Leaving the driver with them, Jack crept along the wall and peered around the corner. Holding up his hand, he folded down his fingers, one by one, as he watched Adèle's movements.

THEY FILED INTO a rectangular foyer, about the size of a large walk-in closet. Against one wall, a row of winter boots was lined neatly on a floor mat beneath a rack of hanging coats. Glancing at the clipboard tacked to the wall opposite the coats, Jack Doherty counted the names printed on the sign-in sheet. Collectively, their eyes fixed upon the windowless door in front of them, its protective barrier, now all that remained in their path. Taking a deep breath, Jack opened it slightly, swept his eyes across the space, and then waved for the others to follow through.

Stepping into the warehouse was an immediate assault on their senses. They stood aghast in sickened silence, covering their faces against the pungent burn of disinfectant. Classical music was playing; the volume was low, and yet, in its melancholy, it seemed to echo the sentiment of the scene before them. Individual perceptions tunneled as their eyes surveyed the layout of the warehouse. The space was vast but the view was unobstructed. Below the rafters and buzzing florescent lights were aisles of caged animals. Their cages were covered with transparent sheeting and stacked one upon the other. Still more were stacked along the loading dock, awaiting transfer. In front of the central row of cages, several white-coated employees were presently seated at a narrow laminate workbench, extending the length of the aisle.

With rage now pounding in his ears like some percussive prelude to battle, Jack recalled the words once spoken to him, albeit under a different set of circumstances:

"No matter how well one prepares oneself to witness the depravity of which mankind is truly capable, there are some imaginings that once realized, forever stamp their horror on one's soul."

He looked at Edward with newfound revulsion, no longer able view him as anything remotely human. Swallowing back the bile rising in his throat, he turned to Adèle. "I need you to stay here and make sure no one tries to leave."

Nodding, she followed his eyes to the backpack slung over her shoulder.

"In the side pocket."

Removing the pistol from the backpack, Adèle reminded herself of what he had said about the blanks. Holding it in the way he had shown her, she stepped to the driver's side.

On Jack's signal, Annick and Mélanie divided, moving quickly along opposite walls towards areas where the lights had been dimmed. When they were in position, he aimed the pistol toward the metal rafters and fired a shot.

"My business is with this man," he called out, pointing the pistol at Edward. "Simply cooperate and you will come to no harm." He then motioned to the area in front of the workbench. "Now, I need all of you to take a seat on the floor here. Find a partner and sit back to back."

The employees remained frozen in place, staring back at him in panic-stricken silence and with fear emblazoned on their eyes. Adèle repeated his instructions, in French; and still no one moved.

"Where the hell did you get these guys from?" said Jack, shoving Edward toward the center of the room.

"THIS ONE'S LOCKED," Annick called out.

Unclasping a key card from an employee's front pocket, Mélanie hurried toward the locked door and held the card in front of the scanner.

Stepping through the door, their eyes were instantly drawn to an anesthetized dog, laying on its side upon a surgical table. On paper sheeting to the left of the table, four newborn puppies were huddled together in a bloody heap. Neither girl dared step closer to confirm what they both were thinking.

In a far corner of the room, a slight man in surgical dress cowered with his hands held over his head. Lunging toward him, Annick pulled him up by his arm. Following her eyes toward the operating table, the color drained from his liver-spotted complexion.

"Is she going to be okay?" Annick held his eyes until he replied with a slight nod.

"And the puppies?"

Looking over at the blood smeared sheet, he muttered something in a language she did not recognize and slowly shook his head. Gesturing his intention, he then walked over to the operating table and proceeded to place the anesthetized dog inside a cage.

NOW SEATED ACROSS from the others, with his ankles bound to the legs of a chair, Edward Blackwell weighed the few options available to him. Outnumbering their captors, they clearly had the advantage. He tried to catch one man's attention and convey what he was thinking, but the man turned his face away.

"I wouldn't do anything stupid if I were you," Adèle called out from across the room.

Jack's head spun around. Meeting Edward's eyes, he clucked his tongue and wagged a cautioning finger. Turning back, he handed the video camera to Annick. "You know what I need you to do?"

Nodding, she took the camera from his hands.

Slowly walking up and down each aisle, Annick filmed the animals in the cages, noting in her hushed commentary the reason behind their silence. She filmed the medical charts and transfer details on the clipboards attached to each cage; she filmed the whiteboard, with its list of surgeries scheduled for the next day; and she filmed the dead puppies, huddled next to the operating table.

Reading the look in her eyes, Jack let his hand rest on hers as he gently removed the camera. "They will pay for this, Annick," he said, holding her eyes. "That much I can promise you."

Nodding, she could not bring herself to speak. Her mouth tasted metallic. She felt like she needed to vomit; like she needed to purge herself of the images she had just captured.

JACK DOHERTY RIPPED the tape off Edward Blackwell's mouth. "Not so intimidating now, are you?" Lighting a cigarette, he took a long drag. "It seems your old man was none too pleased to learn about some of your, how should I put this? Your more, clandestine activities." Tilting his head, he arched his brow and took another drag. "The letter was the least I could do. He had a right to know how you've wasted your life. I'm just grateful I got it to him before it was too late." Dropping the cigarette to the floor, he stubbed it out with the heel of his boot. Then, leaning forward, he rested his elbows on his knees. "You see, Edward, you've become a bit of an obsession of mine." Shaking his head, a gloating smirk set upon his thin red lips. "The truth is, you actually made it quite easy for me. It seems there are no such things as secrets these days, only information waiting to be exposed. A few carefully worded letters sent to the right people and..." Straightening, he snapped his fingers. "Presto."

Turning away, Edward fixed his eyes on the door.

Jack grabbed his chin and forced his face around. "We have a code name for you in our files. Do you want to know what it is?"

Edward grunted.

"Of course you do. Who doesn't want to know their code name? You're called *le chat noir*. Do you want to know why?"

Edward lifted his eyes to the rafters.

"Because cats always manage to land on their feet." Tightening his lips, he snorted a mirthless chuckle. "And my, oh my, if there was any karmic justice in this world you'd have been knocked off your feet years ago."

With his eyes still lifted, Edward breathed an impatient sigh.

"What? You don't believe me? Well, let's see, there's of course the debt of gratitude, you owe to Viktor Toreli." He saw a measure of uncertainty pass over Edward's face. "Well then, allow me to enlighten you. Somehow, he was able to convince his bosses to let him to finish you off, personally. I reckon even you must have realized you were out of your depth with that lot. Guys like that don't play from the same rulebook as your privileged buddies from private school. Attempts to cross them can only ever be resolved in one way, and I assure you it's never pleasant. Though I have to admit, at first, you had me a bit stumped with this one. Why would Viktor Toreli have risked putting his neck on the line like that? But everything finally made sense when I learned about the strings you had pulled to get his brother moved over here. That was smart. You were able to find a weakness and use it to your advantage. Unfortunately, Viktor Toreli was not so lucky. He paid dearly for his betrayal." Lighting another cigarette, he took a couple of long drags, then let it fall from his fingers. Staring down at the floor, he watched as the paper burned to ash, then squished it into the concrete. "Perhaps now, you can begin to see how you are running on borrowed time, my friend. Your fatal flaw is that you've never learned to temper your greed with loyalty. Greed may line your pockets, but it is loyalty that will ultimately save your life."

Slowly, Edward's eyes moved from the video camera to Jack. "If there was any truth to your words, it hardly seems likely I would be sitting here right now."

"The reason you are sitting here right now, is because I decided to take a lesson from your own playbook. It must have driven you crazy, trying to figure out who had sent that letter." Smirking as he leaned back in the chair, Jack crossed his arms and jutted his chin. "Take a look around you, Edward, tonight, another one of your secrets will be revealed."

Heads jolted up at the rhythmic thumping of a helicopter hovering above the facility. Over this, a garbled voice came booming through a loudspeaker outside. Turning to Edward, Jack flashed a smile. "It sounds like an impressive turnout. The cameras will be rolling. I hope you're ready for your close-up."

CHAPTER THIRTY

Walking over to the hostages on the floor, Jack Doherty studied each face carefully as he moved along the aisle. "You," he said, stopping in front of the only female employee. He blinked when she lifted her eyes, wondering whether nature or experience had stamped the bitter scowl onto her face. "Do you understand English?"

She responded with a blank stare.

"I need you to deliver this list of demands to the person in charge out there," he said, holding a piece of paper in front of her face. "Do you understand what I'm saying?"

She nodded, slightly.

Taking out his knife, he cut her loose and pulled her toward the door. "As soon as you get outside, you need to find the person in charge and give them this." He stuffed the folded paper in her lab coat pocket. "Tell them they have thirty minutes. Thirty minutes, got it?"

She inclined her head.

Grabbing the key card from around her neck, he swiped it over the scanner, kicked open the door and shoved her outside.

Before the door slammed shut, he had a split second to glimpse the scene outside. The corners of his mouth upturned. The image captured as a still frame on the lens of his eye. He couldn't blink it away, mesmerized by the splendor of its chaos. Euphoria now coursing through his insides, he turned and stepped back through the door.

"Did you see any media vans?"

Jack shook his head. "They probably have the perimeter cordoned off. But don't worry, Adèle, I think we can rest assured the media's out there." Glancing down at his watch, he noted the time.

BLINDED BY THE assault of white lights, she had no time to react before being forced to the ground by two massive uniforms. She could feel the skin abrading as her chin and knees collided with the gravel. She then felt a weight on her back, pressing down hard and cutting off her airway.

One of the uniforms crouched beside her and patted her down, while the other stood with his firearm pointed at her head. Terrified, her bulging eyes darted. Never before had she seen so many uniforms assembled in one place. Some were standing idle, while others zipped around with determined strides. And there were so many police cars, all parked haphazardly and with their doors left hanging open. She blinked against the spotlights, beaming and streaming with impossible brightness. And those atop cars, their cylindrical rhythm flashing out of phase with the percussive thumping of the helicopter overhead. She gasped as a pair of hands suddenly pulled her to her feet. Her chest heaving, she motioned toward her pocket with her scraped chin.

A third man approached. The addition of his presence—or rather the deferential behavior, it prompted from the other two—afforded a comfort of sorts. She watched his already serious expression become more so as he read over the note. Still, looking at him, she was certain she saw a gentleness behind his pale blue eyes. Though like her own, she could also see the light had long since gone out. She watched as he lifted his arm and made a series of gestures in the direction of the building. The two uniformed men nodded and departed.

Lifting a hand to his brow, he slowly turned.

"Your name?"

"Mina," she said, her voice, like the rest of her body trembling.

"It's okay Mina. You're safe now. I need you to tell me what you can about the situation inside."

She hesitated as her shattered mind worked to translate his

words; and then, slowly, she held up four shaky fingers.

"There are four of them?"

She nodded.

"And how many hostages?"

After another pause, she held up nine fingers.

Pointing to his holster, he said, "Are they armed?"

Following his eyes, she held up two fingers.

"Okay Mina," said Inspector Alain Dalais, waving over a nearby uniform. "One of my officers will escort you down to the station so we can take your statement."

Looking behind her as she was being led away, Mina saw the man with the pale blue eyes standing with his back turned. The two men who had forced her to the ground now stood by his side; other uniforms had gathered around as well, different shades of blacks and blues. Heads nodded as he indicated toward a large sheet of paper, spread open across the hood of a car. She blinked hard, hoping in desperation that when her lids parted, a different reality might meet her eyes. But when her lids parted, the same female officer with the same stoic expression was standing in front of her, holding open the back door of a police cruiser.

FOLDING THE BLUEPRINT, Inspector Alain Dalais stepped inside the mobile command post. Drawing in a deep breath, he picked up the phone; waiting on the line was Director of Police, Arnaud Duclois.

"What are their demands?"

"They want us to send in someone from the media."

"You know we can't do that."

"I know."

"So what are we dealing with here?"

"It's definitely some kind of animal rights group, though I've never heard of them before. There are four of them inside, plus the nine hostages. The hostage, they released saw two firearms."

"Are you still thinking this is related to the other threats we received tonight?"

"It looks that way, probably some kind of diversion."

"A diversion for what exactly?"

"For a public relations nightmare. Their note said the warehouse is being used to quarantine animals brought in through the shelter before they're transported to testing facilities."

The line went silent.

"Sir?"

"Has the negotiator made contact?"

"Their note was explicit, they will not negotiate. It said if we don't have someone from the media inside in," pausing, he glanced at his watch, "twenty minutes, they're going to start on the hostages."

"Who were you thinking?"

"Sergeant Lise Hébert."

"Is she experienced enough to handle something like this?"

"She's the only one with any hope of pulling this off convincingly."

"The name of this group, you said you'd never heard of them before."

"I haven't, no. They signed the note, *Fioretti di San Francesco*."

"*Fioretti di...?* So what you're saying is, we're dealing with a group of *Franciscan* animal rights activists?"

"Right now, the only thing we know for certain is that they're armed and have hostages. We are running a check on the name. I'll let you know if we turn anything up."

CHAPTER THIRTY-ONE

Stopping alongside the police barricade, Sergeant Lise Hébert jumped out of her car and ran over to the QTR news van. "Inside now," she said, locking eyes with Chantal Bélanger.

"What's going on out there Lise?"

"I don't have time to explain. I need to change out of my uniform. Do you have something I can wear?"

Opening a cabinet, Chantal removed a navy blue suit from a hanger and passed it to her.

"That's perfect Chantal, thank you."

"Come on Lise, are you sure there's nothing you can tell me?"

"They want to speak with someone from the media. I won't know more until I get inside." She ran her hands over the slacks to smooth out the creases, then lifted her eyes. "How do I look?"

"Like you chose the wrong profession."

"Thanks Chantal, you're a life saver."

"Lise."

Stopping with her hand on the door, Lise glanced back.

"Be careful, okay."

"I always am."

PULLING OFF TO the side of the road, Sophie parked the car. "I don't think we're going to be able to get much closer," she said, inclining her head toward the police barricade a few kilometers up the road.

Unable to see beyond the massive satellite dishes atop media vans, they stared ahead in silence. A cacophony of garbled sounds projected into the still night air as whirling lights streaked across its charcoal surface. The scene was unnervingly mesmerizing, like some macabre carnival. Crowds of onlookers lined the road. Some were speaking with reporters, while others stood wide-eyed and open-mouthed, wrapping their arms around their children as they craned their necks for a better view.

Turning, Henry Sinclair met her anxious eyes. "Yeah, my gut is telling me the same thing."

"Where to next?"

"Would you mind dropping me off at home?"

"Not at all, but do you think they'll allow you inside?"

"Who?"

"The police. There was a bomb threat at your house, remember?"

DASHING FROM THE command post, Inspector Alain Dalais cut his way through the crowd of officers, to where the paramedics were hurrying an elderly man toward a waiting ambulance. "What the hell happened in there?"

"He's in shock. We need to get him to the hospital."

"Why? What have they done to him?"

"They've cut off his tongue."

The elderly man suddenly lifted his bloodied face. Alain stopped in his tracks. In every respect, both natural and inflicted, the man appeared vampiric. A chill coursed through the marrow of Alain's bones as his thoughts instantly flashed to the fate of the armed officer he had just sent inside. Staring distractedly at the calm urgency of the paramedic's movements, he retraced his mental footsteps, searching for what had led him to make such a grave miscalculation. And just then, he noticed something. "Check his pockets," he called out, rushing forward as the ambulance doors were closing.

With a nod, the blood-spattered pockets of his scrubs were searched. And then, with another nod and a grim expression, the paramedic conveyed to Alain that the missing item had been found.

"There's a note too," she said, crouching down to hand him a folded piece of paper.

Scrawled across the blood-splattered page were the words:

"Atonement made with a tongue.
How many necks on his choice hung?
Justice for all God's creatures or for none.
When the truth is revealed this will be done.

FSF"

CHAPTER THIRTY-TWO

As the ambulance pulled away, Chantal Bélanger locked eyes with Inspector Alain Dalais. She was struggling against the grip of the officer attempting to move her back behind the barricade. "What has happened? Is Lise okay?" she called out, her voice shrill with panic.

Realizing who she was, Alain hurried over. "Give us a minute Rousseau."

Releasing his hold, the officer stepped aside.

"The ambulance was not for Lise," said Alain, keeping his voice low.

Chantal released her breath.

Although still visibly shaken, Alain watched and recognized at once the reflexive change in her mental gears. In an instant she had managed to find her professional voice.

"They knew it was a setup, didn't they?"

He turned as Sergeant Bertrand approached. "The Director is waiting on the phone Alain. This is all over the news."

The sudden explosion lent to their senses the impression the ground was shaking beneath their feet. Limbs extended to brace bodies, panicked eyes darted, and heads jolted toward the direction of the thunderous blast. In the distance, thick gray smoke billowed. From its depths a crimson core raged. Toxic fumes of burning petrol quickly filled the crisp night air.

PULLING INTO THE gas station, Stéphane Brunot turned off his headlights. The road to the north was cordoned off. He could see a helicopter hovering directly above the animal shelter, the white glow of its spotlight threatening the protective cloak of darkness. He was grateful for the wall of media trucks obstructing his view of the shelter, as this meant the reverse would also be true. Still, this did little to steady his nerves or calm his heart, now thumping in his chest like a jackhammer. Stepping inside the payphone booth, he glanced at his watch and waited for Jack's call. The time they had agreed upon came and went. Slowly releasing the air from his lungs, he pushed through the plastic door and walked back to his truck on legs that felt like gelatin.

Blinking away the warning voice in his head, Stéphane began removing the *Jerry Cans* and bales of straw from the back of his truck. After placing fistfuls of straw near the pumps and beneath the propane storage tank, he poured the contents of the *Jerry Cans* along the ground, creating a trail from one site to the next.

At the side of the gas station, a dozen or so cars were parked beneath cheap rainbow bunting, their prices scrawled in yellow across their windshields. Crouching between two cars, Stéphane stretched out his arms, unscrewed the caps, and stuffed a firecracker into the opening of each fuel tank. Rising to his feet, he emptied the last two *Jerry Cans*, continuing the trail of fuel up to each fuse. Then, removing the *Zippo* lighter from his pocket, he flicked it open with his thumb.

CHAPTER THIRTY-THREE

What it was that had caused Jack Doherty to erupt in a violent rage, take out his pocket knife and tear it through the veterinarian's tongue was known to no one in the room, least of all himself. Perhaps the months of planning, sleepless nights, and witnessing of too much senseless cruelty had finally taken its toll. Or perhaps, he had lived too long with the knowledge of how everything that mattered in life could be manipulated to benefit the privileged few who believed themselves untouchable. Or, or, more likely, it was a rage borne of injured pride, unyielding self-righteousness, and the blatant disrespect he had felt at their audacity. To have not only ignored his simple demand, but to have sent her in armed, when they already had a SWAT team in place.

It had required an exhaustive amount of self-control to get him to this point. Ebbs and flows of doubt and certainty, satisfaction and disappointment. And yet, it had only been in that moment, the split-second when he followed her eyes toward the vents, that he had felt a genuine flash of panic. The sudden awareness that just meters away there were police with weapons aimed at him, waiting for the signal to take the shot. Adding to this, though not consciously acknowledged, was the sudden wave uncertainty awoken by his failure to have taken into account the threat posed by those vents.

Blinking hard, he reminded himself it was all about bravado: *Believe it to be so, and it will be so;* and then, slowly releasing a shaky breath, he stepped back through the door. And as his vision tunneled, his determination strengthened, and the belief took hold in his mind. His lip curled in defiance as he gave a sweeping glance across the room, challenging them to take their best shot.

Still gripping the bloodied knife in his trembling hand, he motioned toward the vents and called out, "Everyone make sure you have cover. It appears we have some company."

Fear igniting instinct into action, Adèle darted across the floor. Crouching low, she flicked open her keychain switchblade, and cut Edward's ankles free. Holding the blade below his jaw, she pushed the chair forward with her elbow and reached across to eject the video cassette. With the blade still at his throat, she kept low behind the chair, angling its occupant toward the vents as she back-stepped in the direction of the door. "What are we going to do about him?" she said, slipping the cassette into Jack's pocket.

"If they won't bring the media to us, then we'll just have to go to the media." Tearing his teeth through a strip of duct tape, Jack brushed it across Edward's mouth. He then seized his arms and kicked the chair out from under him, sending it rolling sideways across the concrete floor.

The impact of the explosion sent them reeling.

Bracing himself against Edward's rigid body, Jack's grip tightened. "What the hell did *he* do out there, blow up a munitions factory?"

"I don't know, but—" Adèle's words choked at the sight of the white smoke now filling the room behind them.

Annick raced toward the door with Mélanie at her heels.

Thrusting Edward through the door, Jack shouted, "Run! Go! Now! I'll get their attention."

WITH HIS EYES fixed on the satellite dishes, Jack Doherty ignored the flashing lights, the fire raging in the distance, and the voices calling out for him to drop his weapon. Straining against the efforts of Edward Blackwell's dragging feet, he edged forward along the wall of the building. On the other side of the barricade, the polished media faces watched his approach with a mix of apprehension and eagerness.

What it was he saw in Chantal Bélanger's face that drew him toward her he did not know, something sympathetic perhaps.

Through the darkness and with his own face still covered, he locked her eyes and attempted to convey his intention.

Needing little convincing, Chantal hurdled the barricade. Taking no notice of the commands to stand back, she focused her attention on the masked man with the gun aimed at the hostage.

"Are you going out live?" shouted Jack, his voice garbled by the thumping of the helicopter overhead.

Nodding, she held out her microphone.

"Leave that."

Setting the microphone on the ground, she continued toward him. When only the width of Edward's body stood between them, Jack said, "My pocket."

Reaching inside, her deft fingers managed to quickly tuck the items up her sleeve.

"Guard them with your life."

Although her eyes conveyed to him her understanding, he did not immediately grasp the intent behind the pantomime of her actions.

Moving her hands over the pockets of her suit with the dexterity of seasoned illusionist, she shrugged and shook her head; and then, acting as though she had found the item they were searching for, she eagerly held out a pen.

"More than just a pretty face," he said, his eyes smiling his appreciation.

But what now? Read her expression.

"Write this down on your arm," was his reply:

"'The question is not, can they reason? Nor, can they talk? But can they suffer?'"

A muffled scoff escaped through the tape sealing Edward's lips.

Chantal kept her attention focused on the man with the gun. "Kant?"

"Bentham. Soon you will understand its relevance."

Meeting her eyes as they lifted from her arm, Jack said, "It was never our intention for anyone to get hurt, but the truth must come out."

"I want to hear what you have to say," she said, ignoring the threat behind Edward's piercing stare.

"Get your microphone."

BOLTING DOWN INTO the ravine, they darted into the forest. Adèle Leary quickly lost sight of the others. Running with reckless speed, she zigged and zagged, maneuvering around the trees and tangles of undergrowth. Glimpsing the road, she launched herself through a narrow clearing.

The instant she broke through the woods, she was tackled to the ground. And with her senses taking refuge in its earthy scent, both body and mind shut down; the former now limp and malleable as they cuffed her wrists and yanked her to her feet.

She was only vaguely aware of a hand on her head as the uniforms placed her into the back of the waiting cruiser. She tuned out their actions. She tuned out their words. She tuned out the world.

And as she receded further and further, one thought, one preoccupation still weighed heavy. She whispered his name, envisioning scenarios of his escape. Contented with those thoughts, she allowed numbness to envelop her. Nothing mattered anymore. There was nothing anyone could say or do could hurt her.

CHAPTER THIRTY-FOUR

Panic provided a numbing reprieve for a pain only realized the instant Chantal Bélanger caught sight of the blood, seeping through the tear in her slacks. The microphone fell from her hand. Across from her Jack Doherty was bent over, clutching at his thigh, wincing in pain. Searching frantically through the blinding spotlight of the helicopter overhead, she glimpsed Edward Blackwell being hurried toward a dark SUV. She released her breath. It was over.

A sudden shiver passed over her skin. She froze, choking on her breath as Jack's head flew back. Gasping, gagging, she watched in horror as his body folded to the ground like some tragic marionette whose strings had just been severed. On the gravel beside his head, a pool of blood was forming. She needed to be sick; she needed to scream; she did neither. Her limbs felt leaden, her feet as though embedded in concrete.

Forceful bodies pushed past her as officers swooped down like vultures around his still warm corpse. Her ears ringing with rage, she looked into their faces with a guarded scowl, viewing them with a degree of suspicion beyond that of her journalistic instincts.

The shock induced immobility of mind and limb now lifting, she spun around and darted back toward the barricade. She staggered to a stop as her eyes locked with the man she had spoken to only a short time ago. Defying an almost visceral need to collapse into the arms of the nearest sympathetic body, she straightened her back and jutted her chin and continued toward him.

As she approached, Inspector Alain Dalais eyed her wounded leg with a look of concern. "We should have one of the paramedics take a look at that."

"It's nothing," she said, giving the wound a casual glance. "I must have scraped it on the barricade."

The subtle change in his expression conveyed his thoughts, but he didn't pursue them. "We will need to take your statement."

"I understand, of course, but I am on a deadline. Can I come by the station later tonight?"

"Ask for me," he said, handing her his card.

She glanced at the card, then met his eyes. The question she wanted to ask hung on her lips, but she kept silent. Alain seemed equally tentative, as though he too wanted to say more, but thought better.

"Lise is with the paramedics. She will be fine," he said, his features softening at her reaction to the news.

"Thank you, Inspector."

Taking a step closer, he lowered his voice. "You took something from him out there."

She held his eyes, but did not speak.

"The thing is Mademoiselle Bélanger, if I saw it, then chances are others did as well." Looking down at his hands, Alain paused briefly before adding, "I am going to need something… something I can enter into evidence."

She was silent, her expression guarded.

"Off the record?"

She nodded.

"Something about this whole situation just isn't sitting right with me—" Breaking off, he glanced toward the uniforms now gathered around the body.

"Give me a minute," she said, turning and exchanging an expressive glance with her bewildered cameraman, who, after a moment's hesitation, followed her inside the van.

Returning, she handed Alain a cassette. "It's footage from an exposé we did on puppy mills last year. As I recall, one of our sponsors threatened to pull their ads if we aired it." Pausing, she gave him a half smile. "Politics, you know?" Glancing at the words written on her arm, she added, "But something tells me the subject matter will make a certain kind of sense when this all comes out."

Although he met her words with silence, behind his pale blue eyes, she judged his mind was anything but. Without another word he slowly turned and stepped back over the barricade.

INSPECTOR PIERRE BRODEUR from the *Sûreté du Québec* was now standing over the body of Jack Doherty, instructing two officers with downcast eyes to get the media moved back. Inspector Alain Dalais approached and waited for Pierre to speak.

"Alain, we need to have this area sealed off, it's now a crime scene."

Alain nodded, but did not speak.

"Where's the officer who fired the shots?"

"He's in there waiting for you," said Alain, motioning toward the mobile command post.

"We're going to need his weapon and he will have to be sequestered."

Alain raised his eyes in a manner implying he did not need instruction on protocol. Then, quickly stripping the hostility from his demeanor, he drew a deep breath and said, "The thing is Pierre, his was the shot that hit the victim's leg. I know this guy, he is the best sniper we have. I was standing only a few feet from the scene and I have no idea where that second shot came from."

"Where it came from?" Pierre's eyes narrowed. "Are you saying we don't know who fired the second shot?"

Breathing a heavy sigh, Alain shook his head.

Turning, Pierre considered the body. He then cast a wide glance up to the roof and back down to the parking lot. Meeting Alain's eyes, he said, "You know what I need you to do."

A muffled groan accompanied Alain's reluctant acknowledgement.

"Have them report to SQ headquarters. I give you my assurance they will not be held any longer than is necessary." Looking past Alain, he cocked his head toward the smoke in the distance. "Any word yet on that fire?"

"The suspect is still at large, but we have a description of the vehicle. The propane storage tank must have been overfilled. They think the release valve failed."

"And the hostages?"

"Physically, only cuts and bruises. We are waiting for a translator to take their statements."

"All of them?"

"We suspect they may be here illegally."

"Humph," snorted Pierre, turning as his Sergeant approached.

Listening distractedly to their exchange, Alain glanced around the parking lot, uncertain of what he was hoping to find. Then, turning back, he watched as the same Sergeant gestured to another officer, who then hurried off. Returning a few seconds later, the officer carefully draped a sheet over the body. With Pierre's attention now fully diverted, Alain slipped away without further exchange.

TWO OFFICERS STANDING at the corner of St. Marc and De Maisonneuve motioned for Sophie to turn her car around, their parked cruisers blocking off access.

Henry Sinclair rolled down his window. "But I live on that street," he called out.

One of the officers approached. "May I see some identification?" Giving Henry's license a glance, he asked them to wait and hurried back across the road.

Watching the two officers' exchange words, Henry felt Sophie place her hand reassuringly on his arm, but could not bring himself to turn. Straining his eyes, he searched through the crowd for his brother. It was Walter he saw first.

Hearing Henry's voice call out, they—all three—came running across the street toward Sophie's car. They barely had a chance to speak before Richard, following Henry's eyes, lifted his head from the car window and turned toward the approaching officer.

CHAPTER THIRTY-FIVE

Still not getting an answer on her fifth attempt to call home, Abby Sinclair combed her eyes through the thinning crowd outside the arrivals gate. Holding up the front page of the morning's *Gazette*, James hurried toward her. The phone fell from her hand. "That's our house," she gasped. Her heart racing, she fumbled for the phone, and with trembling fingers dialed her brother's number.

"*WELL, AT LEAST* they're back on the air," said Phillip Madden, his words spoken to James Sinclair over the edge of his coffee cup.

"What do you mean, 'back on the air'?"

"Last night, when the reporter from QTR began her report, the channel went dark."

"It was probably just some sort of technical problem."

"Perhaps, but the timing was a little suspicious."

Looking down the table, James's heart sank as he met Henry's glassy red eyes. "How are you holding up?"

"I still can't get my head around it. I knew Jack was a bit unhinged, but I had no idea he was capable of something like this."

"And the others?"

"Somehow he was able to manipulate them, turn them to his way of thinking." Henry stared into his coffee cup. "How Stéphane looked at me, dad, it was like I no longer recognized him." Breathing a quiet sigh, he lifted his eyes and met his father's directly. "And to think, all this was going on right in front of me, and I didn't see it coming."

"It's not in the nature of honest people to be suspicious when circumstances do not warrant it," said Abby, her features sympathetic as she looked between Henry and Kate; the latter, blinking hard to hold back her tears.

"This is her, Chantal Bélanger, the reporter from last night," said Phillip, motioning for James to turn up the volume.

"*OWNED BY EDWARD* Blackwell, VNP is a private clinical testing laboratory with eight facilities across *Québec*, the largest of which is located on Nun's Island, here in Montréal." Turning, she motioned toward the screen behind her. "The research VNP was hired to conduct on behalf of the clients listed on this slide, was aimed at engineering a new variety of test subjects. This 'next generation' was intended to be streamlined for purpose, while at the same time being altered to such a degree so as to render animal protection legislation inapplicable." Without pause, she motioned to the second slide. "Listed here, are the dates on which secret municipal meetings were held to approve the permits necessary for a private Swiss firm, co-owned by Mr. Blackwell, to construct thirty new animal shelters across *Québec*. Below the dates, are listed the names of the council members in attendance at each of those meetings. Blacked out on the third slide, are the account numbers corresponding to Swiss bank accounts belonging to these same council members. The largest deposits correspond to the dates in which Animal Service contracts between the municipalities and Mr. Blackwell's Swiss firm were signed." Tightening her lips, she set her expression hard. "Over the past two years, a large proportion of the animals in area shelters have suffered through unimaginable acts of cruelty, becoming the unwitting test subjects for the research to which I have referred." Lowering her eyes, she paused briefly. "I have often heard it said that a society can be defined by how well it treats its most vulnerable creatures. Perhaps we need to take a moment and ask ourselves if we want to be defined as a society willing to turn a blind eye to these kinds of practices." Again, she paused briefly. "I must caution that the following footage may be disturbing to some viewers. It contains graphic images of the research being conducted at VNP's facilities, as well as video recorded at one of the shelters where animals were being housed prior to transport. I will report back with more information as soon as it becomes available."

CHAPTER THIRTY-SIX

"You're up early."

"They've issued an arrest warrant for him."

"Edward?"

Nodding, Kate Mironov turned back to the television.

Seating himself across from her, Richard Sinclair lifted his eyes to the screen. He tensed at the footage of protestors lining the barricades in front of VNP's offices, his mind flashing back to the unnerving scene, he had been met with upon his return to work. In front of City Hall, the camera panned along the length of Notre-Dame, focusing on the angry faces, and the placards demanding justice and an end to corruption. At the news desk, the anchor read a statement issued by the police department, cautioning citizens to avoid a list of especially volatile areas. Across the screen flashed a series of images: broken office windows, fires set ablaze in trash cans and projectiles of all sorts being hurled at police in riot gear.

"You still haven't told me why you're up so early," said Richard, reaching for the remote and turning off the television.

"I was thinking I might go in with you today."

"Kate, we've already been through all this."

"But Richard, I've been stuck in this house for days. Don't get me wrong, I appreciate your parents letting me stay here, but I need to get back to work if only for the change of scenery, or else I'm going to lose my mind."

"I understand, but you've seen for yourself what a mess it is down by the office. A group of them had Uncle Phillip and I trapped in his car for half an hour. Please, Kate, just give it a couple more days for things to settle down."

"Couple of days? You heard them, Richard, warrants and independent inquiries. This is going to go on for months."

Neither said another word. A brief silence passed with him deliberately avoiding her eyes as she moved to search his out. Then, standing up from the table, he walked over to the patio door and picked up his backpack. Breathing a reluctant sigh, he glanced back over his shoulder.

"Alright, but if I see any protestors in the parking lot, I'm turning the car around."

WITH THE SCALPEL resting impossibly close to the anesthetized rat's taut skin, Richard Sinclair hesitated, unable to make the incision. Relaxing his hand, he set the scalpel down, and pulled the surgical mask over his head. It was no use, he told himself; once again confronted with the burden of responsibility that had been hampering him all week. It was a preoccupation made more pronounced by the impulse to glance over his shoulder every few seconds, anxious some masked vigilante might appear out of nowhere when his back was turned.

Prior to Monday night, his only personal experience with the other side of the debate had ever been through conversations with his brother. Conversations which invariably ended with neither much swayed by the other's arguments. But now, there was no denying that something within him had been altered by the grotesque images of torture, captured to memory from the television screen. He wondered if these feelings would pass. He wondered if others like him had been similarly affected by those images. He wondered if, when all the dust had settled, anything will have changed. And just then, as his eyes connected with the clock on the wall, an unnerving chill tore through his insides, bringing his introspection to an abrupt end.

"IS KATE UP there with you?"

"Kate? No. Why?"

"She went to get coffee over an hour ago and hasn't come back."

"Okay," sighed Phillip Madden. "Sit tight, I'll go and have a look around."

Richard dove for the phone when it rang.

"Alex said he hasn't seen her since she left to find you."

"Dammit. I knew I shouldn't have let her come today."

"Don't jump to conclusions, Richard. Perhaps she went across the street for coffee. You know what they're like at that café, always gossiping about something or other."

"She didn't take her purse."

Phillip was silent.

"I can't explain it, uncle, I just know something's wrong. I can feel it in my bones."

"Have you called home?"

"Home? Why?" he snapped. "She doesn't have dementia. She's hardly just going to get up and leave without telling me." The words had barely passed his lips before his cracking voice faltered through an apology.

"There's no need to apologize, Richard, I understand. Tell me what you need me to do."

"If she returns while I'm out looking for her, please, just make sure she stays put until I get back."

PLACING THE PHONE on speaker, Phillip Madden hesitated at the silence with which his words were met. Swallowing, he repeated his question: "Any luck?"

"No, it's like she's vanished; and I spoke to Henry and he hasn't heard from her either."

"Okay, I'll call the security company."

"And what? I tried speaking with the guard at the front door and he was useless."

"The feed from the camera outside is recorded on a twelve hour loop. I will have them check through it for anything suspicious."

STARING DOWN AT the card of the officer who had questioned him on Monday night, Richard Sinclair reached an unsteady hand for the phone.

Inspector Alain Dalais picked up on the first ring.

"My name is Richard Sinclair. I'm not sure if you remember me, but…"

"Sinclair, yes, I remember. Please tell me you're calling with information on the whereabouts of Edward Blackwell."

"I'm calling because one of our staff has gone missing."

"Missing? How long have they been missing?"

"A few hours."

"I see. Well, an adult missing for a few hours is usually not cause for alarm."

"I understand, and believe me, sir, I wouldn't have called unless I was certain something had happened to her. We've searched the building several times. She went upstairs for coffee and never came back. She didn't take her purse with her. And there have been protestors out front all week. The kind of protestors who, my gut is telling me, may have decided to follow through on the threats they were making."

Alain was silent for a short time as he considered Richard's words. Though he could not understand why—as experience dictated otherwise—his instincts were sounding their intuitive alert; and both mind and conscience were telling him to err on the side of caution. He breathed a heavy sigh. "Do you have a recent photo?"

"Let me check." Reaching for her purse, Richard flipped through her wallet. "Yes, there's her driver's license and a family photo."

"Okay. Try to put together a detailed timeline of her movements leading up to her disappearance. I will be there shortly."

Hanging up the phone, Richard closed his eyes and pictured Kate as she was when she had left. He had barely glanced up as her lips brushed against his cheek.

"Be back in a sec.," she had said.

He could hear her voice so clearly, it was as though she was standing right in front of him. It was unbearable. The rawness of the pain was visceral, like sharpened claws tearing his insides to shreds. The sense of foreboding was one not unfamiliar to him; and now, as with the time before, it hung over him like a storm cloud, foretelling with equal certainty that tragedy was imminent.

CHAPTER THIRTY-SEVEN

"Kate!"

Calling out her name, Richard Sinclair sprang out of the chair and raced to open the door.

"Sorry Richard, my hands were full. I brought you down some food." Setting the bag down on the workbench, Phillip hesitated, unsure of what to say or do. With his arms crossed, he stood still and silent, watching from beneath his brow as Richard paced the floor. The despairing internal monologue, laid bare in his nephew's altering expression, was as difficult to witness as it was to interrupt. "I spoke to the security company," he said, quietly.

Richard stopped in his tracks. "And?"

Tightening his lips, Phillip slowly shook his head.

Richard took his head in his hands. "But I don't understand. I've looked everywhere, she still can't be in the building."

They both froze at the faint sound of tapping on the door.

"Yes," said Phillip, motioning for Richard to wait.

When no one answered Phillip moved toward the door. Pausing, he glanced back, and in Richard's anxious expression saw reflected the internal alarm his own instincts were sounding.

"Who's there?" Phillip's hand now gripped the handle. Casting another glance back, he mouthed for Richard to dial the police. Then, steadying his footing, he slowly opened the door. Shock stalled his reflexes. "What the...? But, how...?" he gasped, reeling as Edward Blackwell forced his way inside.

Dropping the phone, Richard lunged at Edward, colliding with his right arm just as he was moving to rip the cord from the wall. For a split-second their eyes locked: Richard's bewilderment confronting Edward's menacing smirk. Then, lowering his eyes, Richard gasped, panic-stricken at the sight of the syringe in Edward's left hand. Staggering back, Richard lifted his shirt, swallowing against the pain induced queasiness rising in his throat.

Rushing to his side, Phillip's stomach plunged at the sight of the silver tip, embedded in his skin. Tearing the first aid kit off the wall, he rifled through the plastic box, returning with a pair of tweezers. Spreading out the skin around the puncture, he secured the tip of the needle and carefully eased it out. Helping him into a chair, he held his eyes in a silent exchange, before turning to face Edward.

Silent, disheveled and savage, Edward's eyes glazed and glinted as he stared across at Richard in a trance of maniacal wonderment. Then, slowly, his features sharpened; and as his eyes met Phillip's directly, they flashed in vengeful triumph.

"Think for a minute," he whispered. "Are you not the one who is always speaking about the balance of nature? Surely, you of all people can appreciate the symmetry of my actions."

After a split second hesitation, Phillip sprang for the refrigerator door.

"Not so fast, Phillip. That is, unless you have no interest in the fate of the girl."

"No," wailed Richard, lurching, wincing, faltering and collapsing back into the chair.

Phillip held his desperate eyes briefly before turning back to Edward.

"I am pleased you have decided to see things my way," said Edward, forcing solemnity into his silken tone. He stared down at his hands. Then, fiddling with his signet ring, he quietly said, "At first my father's betrayal weighed heavily upon my mind." His eyes, now questioning, shifted toward Phillip. "How could it not?" He looked back down at his ring. "But what my father failed to recognize was that I never had a choice. One's actions are only wrong if they betray one's true nature. And thus, for me to have existed in any other manner would have been unnatural, a betrayal unto nature itself." Clasping his hands, he tented his fingers and pointed them at Phillip. "You on the other hand, you recognized the weakness in my character and chose to abandon me, siding with that imposter and sentencing me to a life without love, without compassion and hope." Tilting his head, he narrowed his eyes and studied Phillip's unyielding features. "You do see how you have only yourself to blame for your current predicament?"

Phillip's stony expression conveyed his silent loathing as he moved to Edward's side. "I was there that day remember," he said, his voice low and cutting. "That day, when I had to pick my sister's battered body up from the bedroom floor."

Looking beyond him, Edward's lips tightened as he inclined his head toward Richard. It was a look of rebuke, a warning, a reminder, lest he forget just who was in control at that moment. Taking a step back, Phillip swallowed hard against the surge of rage. "What is it you want Edward?" The words scraped against his tightly clenched jaw.

Reaching into his jacket pocket, Edward handed him an envelope. "What are you waiting for you fool? Open it. The clock is ticking."

Straightaway Phillip doubted its legitimacy. The one-page document was printed on the flimsy letterhead of a Montréal law firm he had never heard of. It was as though some coerced lawyer had drawn it up to oblige Edward, while deliberately ensuring its contents would never see the light of day. If he had needed any further confirmation that Edward had gone completely mad, then the document in his hands was it. Guarding his thoughts, he lifted his eyes over the paper. "You are delusional," he scoffed, channeling his fury into a tone of indignation. "There's no way you are getting your hands on those drugs."

"Very well, if the drugs are worth more to you than her life, then so be it. The choice is yours."

Using his last ounce of self-control, Phillip grabbed the pen from Edward's outstretched hand."

"See, now that wasn't so difficult," said Edward, glancing at the signature as he tucked the document back into the envelope, and the envelope back into his jacket pocket.

Just then it happened, as though on cue, that Richard released a pained moan. And in the instant it took Phillip to glance over his shoulder, Edward sprang for the door.

Lunging at him, Phillip forced him against the wall. "Where is she?" he growled, tightening his grip as he stared down hard into the soulless eyes of a psychopath.

CHAPTER THIRTY-EIGHT

Inspector Alain Dalais descended the darkened stairwell with his senses heightened and his footing cautious. Perspiration peppered his brow as he edged along the wall toward the horizontal beam of light, projecting from beneath the door. Tilting his ear toward the jamb, he strained to make clear the muffled voices on the other side. With his back pressed flat against the concrete wall and his pulse racing, he slowly released his breath and drew his sidearm.

"IT IS INTERESTING how neither of them have developed a cough. Though, perhaps that is down to the route of entry." Edward Blackwell's tone was perversely contemplative as he stared at Richard with an expression of depraved curiosity. "I admit it was not my finest hour, but you must understand, I had to act quickly." Vile satisfaction glinted in his eyes as they lifted and locked with Phillip's. "Then again, there is a certain irony to it, her location I mean; that is to say, if you consider it in relation to the events of this past week."

Phillip held his eyes for the moment it took to untwist his twisted words. Then, releasing his grip, he spun around and raced to the refrigerator.

With his instinct to flee now hindered by his stronger drive to seek pleasure in another's suffering, Edward stood motionless, mesmerized by the desperation of Phillip's darting motions. He noted the color draining from his complexion, the perspiration on his upper lip, and the tremble in his hands as he tore through the courier label and ripped off the lid of the *Styrofoam* cooler.

Removing two vials, Phillip rushed over to Richard's side. He gently tilted back his nephew's feverish head and emptied the contents of the vial down his throat. Then, without pause for thought, he sprinted toward the door.

Hearing the turn of the handle, Inspector Alain Dalais kicked open the door, sending Phillip stumbling back.

"I… I have to go and…" stammered Phillip, holding out the vial in his trembling hand.

Alain moved aside to let him pass. He then reached for his handcuffs, and stepping cautiously toward Edward, proceeded to secure him to the radiator.

AT THE BACK of the small room, tucked behind a tall shelving unit, whereupon caged rats scurried about their shavings, was Kate Mironov's lifeless body. Clutching the vial in his sweat-soaked palm, Phillip Madden crouched down beside her and felt for a pulse. It was faint. Sharp stabs of pain choked his breath for the split second it took for the reflexive action to move the liquid down her throat. Draping her body in his arms, he hurried back up the corridor.

"The ambulance is on its way."

"Okay," said Phillip, through a winded breath, his limbs weak and shaking as he gently placing her limp body down in a chair next to Richard, "we need to try and get her temperature lowered before her organs start shutting down." Rushing to the freezer, he slid a box of latex gloves across the workbench toward Inspector Alain Dalais. "Here, you'd better put these on."

Peeling Kate's blouse away, Phillip emptied the contents of the ice box over her sweat-soaked crimson skin; while Alain, standing with his arms outstretched between her and Richard, held ice-packs to their foreheads. Lifting Richard's burning wrist, Phillip checked his pulse. It was still strong. Releasing a shaky breath, he was suddenly gripped by a stabbing pain in his chest. His heart felt as though it was in a tightening vice-grip. Clutching his arm, he winced through the sharpening stabs now accompanying his every inhalation. Turning away from Alain's questioning stare, he moved toward the refrigerator.

"Are you okay?"

"I'm fine. Whatever it was, it's now passed," said Phillip, handing Alain a vial.

"What's this?"

"It's highly unlikely you have been exposed, but we cannot afford to take any chances."

Lifting his panic-stricken eyes, Alain looked between Richard and Kate, and then back at Phillip. Without pausing to give voice to the trepidation reading plainly on his face, he uncapped the vial and drank its contents.

The hard leather soles upon which Phillip stood, flinched against the urge to unleash their fury as he glared down at Edward, deliberating. Yielding to circumstance, he bent down and placed the vial into the palm of Edward's free hand. Staring down at the vial, Edward appeared almost childlike in his confusion.

"You either take it yourself or I will force it down your throat. Believe me, I could care less about your welfare, but we need to keep this contained." Turning back to Alain, Phillip answered his still unvoiced question. "He has injected them with a mutant strain of a bacteria that causes TB."

The vial fell from Alain's hand. He searched to retrieve what little he knew about tuberculosis; grainy images of patients in sanatoriums clouded his eyes. His mouth opened, but fearing the answer he might receive, his words stuck in his throat.

"The medicine is a precaution only."

Alain looked between Richard and Kate. "Are... Are they going to be okay?"

Phillip did not answer.

They both turned toward the sound of the approaching sirens.

"Can you help me carry them to the door? We need to keep traffic in here to a minimum."

Nodding, Alain stepped toward Kate and collected her into his arms. Turning his face away, he shuddered at the intense heat radiating off her fever-ravished skin; their efforts having done little to bring her temperature down.

Minutes later, the ambulance tore out of the lot, its blaring sirens piercing through the still night air.

LISTENING CAREFULLY AS Phillip Madden spoke, the doctors kept their thoughts guarded.

"From what we have observed so far, the efficacy of the phages appears to decrease if administered four hours after initial exposure to the pathogen," continued Phillip, wringing his hands as he followed them off the elevator.

"How much time has elapsed since they were infected?"

"Richard, approximately two hours and Kate," he paused, "I cannot say for certain," he swallowed, "worse case, between six and eight hours."

"Okay, we will take it from here.

Phillip stood motionless, watching as the gurneys were hurried down the corridor. He turned with a start when a nurse approached.

"You can wait over here, sir," she said, her voice low and gentle as she motioned to a chair across from the nurse's station.

"Is there a phone I can use?"

"You may use the phone at the nurses' station."

Holding her warm gray eyes, his features suddenly locked in panic and pained confusion. An expression of terror froze upon the pallid canvass of his face like some tragic death mask; and then, with his hand clutching his arm, he fell to his knees.

CHAPTER THIRTY-NINE

"Have you taken his statement?"

"He's been processed, but said he would only speak to you directly. He's refused a lawyer."

"Any word from the hospital?"

"They were able to stabilize the man, but the woman's condition is still critical."

Blinking, Director of Police Arnaud Duclois took a step back. "Should you even be here?"

Pulling up his sleeve, Inspector Alain Dalais showed him the small puncture from the skin test. "They say they'll know for certain in forty-eight hours. But my understanding is, if I had been infected, I wouldn't be standing here right now."

Arnaud breathed a heavy sigh. The waft of tobacco told of his having had yielded to a habit long ago abandoned. Alain studied his face closely, searching for some indication of what he was thinking. The telling lines now more pronounced, Arnaud looked as though he had aged ten years over the course of the past week.

"Do you have any idea why he is asking for you?"

"I imagine he thinks I can do something to make this go away."

Handing him the file, Alain grunted. "The way he's acting, my guess is he's trying to lay the groundwork for an insanity defense."

"Thank you Alain. You have done well." Opening the file, Arnaud eyed the pages carefully. "Okay," he said, through another sigh, "let's see what he has to say for himself."

"Do you want me in there with you?"

Arnaud shook his head. "This conversation shouldn't take too long. Regardless of what he thinks, he is not above procedure."

EDWARD BLACKWELL'S HEAD shot up when Director of Police Arnaud Duclois entered. "You certainly took your time."

Pulling out the chair across from him, Arnaud sat down. Resting his elbows on the table, he clasped his hands in front of him and gave Edward a measured look.

"How long before I am released?"

Tilting his head, Arnaud narrowed his eyes. "That is not likely to happen. You are considered too much of a flight risk."

"I see."

"You know Edward, you really dropped us in it with that situation down at the shelter."

Though Edward's demeanor was unyielding in its composure, he flinched slightly when Arnaud suddenly brought his fist down on the table.

"Goddammit Edward, you could have at least tried to cover your tracks. And what you did last night—" Breaking off, he met Edward's impassive eyes directly. "You do realize you have been charged with two counts of attempted murder."

Aside from the faint involuntary twitches, Edward remained perfectly still, his dark eyes slowly glazing over.

"The thing is Edward, through your reckless actions, you have placed us in an impossible situation." He drew back as Edward's eyes suddenly sparked to life, flashing a savage glint.

"Please Arnaud, I have one hell of a headache and could really do without the theatrics." He stared down at his signet ring. "I appreciate I may have ruffled a few feathers, but let's not waste time with idle threats, we both know you will find a way to get me out of here."

"Are you sure about that?"

Lifting his eyes, he searched Arnaud's face for some indication he was bluffing, but found none. "I see," he muttered, folding his hands across his chest. "And was everyone in agreement?"

"It was unanimous."

Edward grunted.

"They feel you have become too much of a liability, and that assisting you now is a risk they are unwilling to take." Pausing, he ran a hand across his brow and slowly shook his head. "You have no idea how close you came to being left in that Mozambican prison cell." Again he shook his head. "I am sorry Edward, but you have brought this upon yourself. You allowed your personal feelings to cloud your judgment."

"My father always spoke highly of you Arnaud. He even went so far as to defend your decision to join the police force to your father." Pausing, he held Arnaud's eyes. "Oh, I see you didn't know about that. It was he who convinced your father not to cut you off. The old fool; going on and on about how it would shield you from corruption. How little he knew about how things truly operate."

"Please Edward, I need you to listen to me carefully—" Breaking off, Arnaud stared into his clasped hands, searching for the most tactful way to say what needed to be said. Then, slowly lifting his eyes, he met Edward's directly. They now appeared genuinely withdrawn, his demeanor subdued. Arnaud released a quiet breath. He had been prepared to have his words met with resistance, but the man now before him appeared as one reconciled to his fate.

"So this is how it ends," said Edward, his voice a solemn whisper.

"It is an honorable end. And you can rest assured we will do what we can to portray your legacy in a similar light."

Lowering his eyes, Edward was silent. *An honorable end.* In his mind, he scoffed at the notion. They both knew his acquiescence was not borne from any sense of honor. One way or the other, they were not going to allow this case to go to trial. Better to end things cleanly here and now with a bullet, than with a makeshift weapon in some godforsaken prison.

"And the child?"

"She will be protected."

"I will hold you to that."

Swallowing, Arnaud expressed his next words without speaking.

Again Edward's eyes glazed over as he envisioned the chilling scene that was to follow. A shiver ran through his body: the surreal sensation of witnessing one's own death minutes before it was about to occur. Slowly, his glance shifted toward the ceiling. "What are you going to do about the camera?"

"It's been taken care of."

"Of course it has. Well then, I imagine we had better make it look convincing."

"Yes, we best."

Rising from his chair, Arnaud removed his sidearm and placed it on the table. He then walked over to Edward and nodded. With his fist clenched behind his back, Edward slowly rose to his feet. And as their eyes locked in a silent exchange, he swung it into Arnaud's jaw. Arnaud stumbled back. Through his muted groan, he motioned to his side. Edward's still clenched fist landed a second punch below Arnaud's rib cage. Keeling over, Arnaud clutched at his stomach, gasping for air.

Turning his back, the pistol now in his hand, Edward waited. After a few seconds, he glanced over his shoulder and nodded. Still bent over and struggling to catch his breath, Arnaud gathered his strength and charged at him, knocking him to the floor. He could hear the sound of feet rushing to the door. Now face to face on the floor, the two men grappled for the weapon.

The door flew open.

"Drop the weapon," shouted Inspector Alain Dalais, standing in the doorway with his sidearm drawn.

In an instant the pistol turned.

"Don't do this Edward," gasped Arnaud, meeting his desperate eyes as they exchanged a final glance.

Edward's finger pulled on the trigger.

"No!" Arnaud's agonizing cry tore through the room, freezing its stunned occupants in place.

His chest heaving, Arnaud propped himself up on his elbows; then, gripping Edward's wrist, he checked for a pulse.
Stepping forward, Alain placed a hand on his shoulder. Arnaud's head swung around. With his eyes ablaze, he cast a frantic look at Alain. Lowering his head, Alain took a step back. Turning, Arnaud gently closed the blood splattered lids of Edward's lifeless eyes, silently wishing him the peace in death that had so long eluded him in life.

CHAPTER FORTY

Sitting in front of the observation window, Richard Sinclair reached for his IV and adjusted the morphine. Mercifully, his thoughts soon drifted back to that night at the opera; to how intoxicating he had found the very rhythm of her breath. He remembered thinking it a peculiar thing to marvel at, and yet now, he would trade anything and everything to live with her forever in the ecstasy of that singular moment.

Glimpsing the night sky through the tiny window of her hospital room, he narrowed his eyes and stared out at the stars; then, fixing upon the brightest, he wondered if it was possible that wherever she was, she might be gazing upon the same star. Though he knew it was a ridiculous thought, he nonetheless clung to it, dreaming of the possibility that two people, unfathomable lengths apart might be united in the shared experience of a singular and brilliant pinhole of light. Blinking, he shook his head. The action sent a sharp shock of pain coursing around his skull. Again he adjusted his morphine.

Looking over his shoulder, his eyes followed the thin black arm of the institutional clock on the wall, watching as it ticked away the minutes. Then, closing his eyes, he attempted to piece together the fragments he could remember. But it was all still a blur of impressions. He winced as another sharp stab of pain brought with it an impenetrable blackness. When the severe throbbing had eased to a tolerable pulse, he slowly lifted his lids. Though as he did so, the combined effects of morphine, flickering fluorescent lights and industrial cleaning solution made him feel like he was going to vomit.

Start with what you remember.

He recalled hearing the doctors' voices shortly after regaining consciousness. The words were garbled and the faces blurred, but he was certain he had heard one of them speak his uncle's name. He remembered looking between them in pleading silence, unable to find his voice; and then came the sensation he was drowning; and then darkness.

Why won't anyone tell me anything?

He turned back toward the observation window. He sat for some time, staring through the glass, lost in the memories of happy times. His thoughts were interrupted by the sound of the nurse's voice.

What had she said her name was?

"Tomorrow you will be allowed visitors," she said, her gentle voice low and soothing.

Staring ahead, he did not reply.

"She is stable," she added, following his eyes. "But I am afraid her condition remains unchanged. It is going to take some time for her body to recover. But I can tell she is a fighter."

Her round and friendly face offered him a reassuring smile. He wanted desperately to believe what he saw in her eyes.

"Thank you," he mouthed, forcing a weak smile as he turned back to the observation window.

AND AS THE minutes turned to hours, and the hours to days, there he would remain, until he did no longer; seated in front of her window, outside looking in, dreaming and hoping and escaping to the serenity of happy memories, blissfully relived again and again.

The Scientist

CPSIA information can be obtained at www.ICGtesting.com
Printed in the USA
LVOW04s2108010115

421099LV00029B/920/P

9 781499 730357